29/4/17

SPECIAL MESSAGE TO READERS

THE ULVERSCROFT FOUNDATION
(registered UK charity number 264873)
was established in 1972 to provide funds for research, diagnosis and treatment of eye diseases. Examples of major projects funded by the Ulverscroft Foundation are:-

- The Children's Eye Unit at Moorfields Eye Hospital, London
- The Ulverscroft Children's Eye Unit at Great Ormond Street Hospital for Sick Children
- Funding research into eye diseases and treatment at the Department of Ophthalmology, University of Leicester
- The Ulverscroft Vision Research Group, Institute of Child Health
- Twin operating theatres at the Western Ophthalmic Hospital, London
- The Chair of Ophthalmology at the Royal Australian College of Ophthalmologists

You can help further the work of the Foundation by making a donation or leaving a legacy. Every contribution is gratefully received. If you would like to help support the Foundation or require further information, please contact:

THE ULVERSCROFT FOUNDATION
The Green, Bradgate Road, Anstey
Leicester LE7 7FU, England
Tel: (0116) 236 4325

website: www.foundation.ulverscroft.com

Anne Perry is a *New York Times* bestselling author noted for her memorable characters, historical accuracy and exploration of social and ethical issues. Her two series, one featuring Inspector Thomas Pitt and one featuring Inspector William Monk, have been published in multiple languages. She has also published a successful series based around World War One and the Reavley family. Anne Perry was selected by *The Times* as one of the twentieth century's '100 Masters of Crime' and now lives in Scotland.

A CHRISTMAS GARLAND

1857: Lieutenant Victor Narraway arrives at a battered military base at Cawnpore just two weeks before Christmas, but no one is celebrating: they have been betrayed. A soldier under arrest for dereliction of duty killed a guard and escaped to join the rebels, taking crucial information that led to the massacre of nine men on patrol. Someone must have helped him, and medical orderly John Tallis is the only man unaccounted for at the time. He is now on trial for his life, and Narraway is commanded to defend him. The British Army needs justice to be carried out in full, and there seems no doubt of Tallis's guilt. But Narraway cannot see any motive for his actions. Will an innocent man hang before Christmas?

ANNE PERRY

A CHRISTMAS GARLAND

Complete and Unabridged

CHARNWOOD
Leicester

First published in Great Britain in 2012 by
Headline Publishing Group
An Hachette UK Company
London

First Charnwood Edition
published 2013
by arrangement with
Headline Publishing Group
An Hachette UK Company
London

A catalogue record for this book is available
from the British Library.

ISBN 978–1–4448–1773–7

Published by
F. A. Thorpe (Publishing)
Anstey, Leicestershire

Set by Words & Graphics Ltd.
Anstey, Leicestershire
Printed and bound in Great Britain by
T. J. International Ltd., Padstow, Cornwall

This book is printed on acid-free paper

For all those who keep hope alive
in the darkness

Lieutenant Victor Narraway walked across the square in the cool evening air. It was mid-December, a couple of weeks before Christmas. At home in England it might already be snowing, but here in India there would not even be a frost. No one had ever seen snow in Cawnpore. Any other year it would be a wonderful season: one of rejoicing, happy memories of the past, optimism for the future, perhaps a little nostalgia for those one loved who were far away.

But this year of 1857 was different. The fire of mutiny had scorched across the land, touching everything with death.

He came to the outer door of one of the least-damaged parts of the barracks and knocked. Immediately it was opened and he stepped inside. Oil lamps sent a warming yellow light over the battered walls and the few remnants of the once secure occupation, before the siege and then its relief a few months ago. There was little furniture left whole: a bullet-scarred desk, three chairs that had seen better days, a bookcase and several cupboards, one with only half a door.

Colonel Latimer was a tall and spare man well into his forties. A dozen Indian summers had burned his skin brown, but there was little colour beneath it to give life to the weariness and the

1

marks of exhaustion. He regarded the twenty-year-old lieutenant in front of him with something like apology.

'I have an unpleasant duty for you, Narraway,' he said quietly. 'It must be done, and done well. You're new to this regiment, but you have an excellent record. You are the right man for this job.'

Narraway felt a chill, in spite of the mildness of the air. His father had purchased a commission for him and he had served a brief training in England before being sent out to India. He had arrived a year ago, just before the issue of the fateful cartridges at Dum Dum in January, which later in the spring had erupted in mutiny. The rumour had been that they were covered in animal grease in the part required to be bitten in order to open them for use. The Hindus had been told it was beef fat. Cows were sacred and to kill one was blasphemy. To put the fat to the lips was damnation. The Muslims had been told it was pork fat, and the pig was an unclean animal. To put that grease to your lips would damn your soul, although for an entirely different reason.

Of course, that was not the cause of the mutiny by hundreds of thousands of Indians against the rule of a few thousand Englishmen employed by the East India Company. The real reasons were more complex, far more deeply rooted in the social inequities and the cultural offences of a foreign rule. This was merely the spark that had ignited the fire.

Also it was true, as far as Narraway could

gather, that the mutiny was far from universal. It was violent and terrible only in small parts of the country. Thousands of miles were untouched by it, lying peaceful, if a little uneasy, under the winter sun.

But the province of Sind on the Hindustan plains had seen much of the very worst of it, Cawnpore and Lucknow in particular.

General Colin Campbell, a hero from the recent war in the Crimea, had fought his way through to relieve the siege at Lucknow. A week ago he had defeated 25,000 rebels here at Cawnpore. Was it the beginning of a turning in the tide? Or just a glimmer of light that would not last?

Narraway stood to attention, breathing deeply to calm himself. Why had he come to Latimer's notice?

'Yes, sir,' he said between his teeth.

Latimer smiled bleakly. There was no light in his face, no warmth of approval. 'You will be aware of the recent escape of the prisoner Dhuleep Singh,' he went on. 'And that in order to achieve it the guard Chuttur Singh was hacked to death.'

Narraway's mouth was dry. Of course he knew it; everyone in the Cawnpore station knew it.

'Yes, sir,' he said obediently, forcing the words out.

'It has been investigated.' Latimer's jaw was tight; a small muscle jumped in his temple. 'Dhuleep Singh had privileged information regarding troop movements, specifically the recent patrol that was massacred. The man could not have escaped without assistance.' His voice was growing quieter, as if he found the words more and more difficult to say. He cleared his throat with an effort. 'Our enquiries have excluded every possibility, except that he was helped by Corporal John Tallis, the medical orderly.' He met Narraway's eyes. 'We will try him the day after tomorrow. I require you to speak in his defence.'

Narraway's mind whirled. There was a chill like ice in the pit of his stomach. A score of reasons leaped to his mind why he could not do what Latimer was asking of him. He was not even remotely equal to the task. It would be so much better to have one of the officers who had been with the regiment during the siege and the relief, and who knew everyone. Above all, they should have an officer who was experienced in military law, who had done this dozens of times, and was known and respected by the men.

Then a cold, sane voice inside assured him that it was precisely because he was none of these things that Latimer had chosen him.

'Yes, sir,' he said faintly.

'Major Strafford will be here any moment,' Latimer continued. 'He will give you any instruction and advice that you may need. I shall be presiding over the court, so it is not appropriate that I should do it.'

'Yes, sir,' Narraway said again, feeling as if another nail had been driven into the coffin lid of his career. Major Strafford's dislike of him dated from before the time he had joined the regiment. Almost certainly it came from

Narraway's brief acquaintance with Strafford's younger brother. They had been in the same final year at Eton, and little about their association had been happy.

Narraway had been academic, a natural scholar and disinclined towards sports. The younger Strafford was a fine athlete, but no competition for Narraway in the classroom. They existed happily enough in a mutual contempt. It was shattered one summer evening in a magnificent cricket match, nail-bitingly close but Strafford's team having the edge, until Narraway showed a rare flash of brilliance in the only sport he actually enjoyed. The dark, slender scholar, without a word spoken, bowled out the last three men in Strafford's team, including the great sportsman himself. The fact that he did it with apparent ease was appalling, but that he did not overtly take any pleasure in it was unforgivable.

Strafford Minor had never been able to exact his revenge in the field, which was the only place where he could redeem his honour. Other quarrels or victories did not count. No practical joke or barbed wit looked anything better than the spite of a bad loser.

But that was boyhood, two years ago and thousands of miles away.

'Captain Busby will prosecute,' Latimer was going on. 'The evidence seems simple enough. You will be free to interview Corporal Tallis at any time you wish, and anyone else you feel could be helpful to your defence. Any legal points that you need clarifying, speak to Major Strafford.'

'Yes, sir.' Narraway was still at attention, his muscles aching with the effort of keeping complete control of himself.

There was a brief knock on the door.

'Come,' Latimer ordered.

The door swung open and Major Strafford came in. He was a tall, handsome man in his early thirties, but the echo of Narraway's schoolfellow, so much his junior, was there in the set of his shoulders, the thick, fair hair, the shape of his jaw.

Strafford glanced at Latimer.

'Sir.' He saluted, then, as he was given permission, relaxed. He regarded Narraway expressionlessly. 'You'd better read up on it tonight and start questioning people tomorrow morning,' he said. 'You need to be sure of the law. We don't want anyone afterwards saying that we cut corners. I presume you appreciate that?'

'Yes, sir.' Narraway heard the edge of condescension in Strafford's voice and would dearly like to have told him that he was as aware as anyone else of how they would all be judged on their conduct in the matter. More than that, the future of British rule in India would be flavoured by report of decisions such as this. The whole structure of Empire hung together on the belief in justice, in doing things by immutable rules and a code of honour that they themselves never broke.

Thousands of men were dead already, as well as women and children. If they ever regained control and there were to be any kind of peace, it must be under the rule of law. It was the only safety for people of any colour or faith. Once they themselves gave in to barbarism there was no hope left for anyone. Right now, there seemed to be little enough in any circumstances. Delhi had fallen, Lucknow, Agra, Jhelum, Sugauli, Dinapoor, Lahore, Kolapore, Ramgarh, Peshawar — and on and on. The list seemed endless. Perhaps there was nothing left but some shred of honour.

'Good,' Strafford said curtly. 'Whatever you think you know, you'd better come and see me and tell me at least the outline of your defence.' He looked at Narraway closely, his blue eyes curiously luminous in the light of the oil lamp. 'You must be sure to mount some defence, you do understand that, don't you? At least put forward a reason why a man like Tallis should betray the men he's served beside all his career. I know he's quarter Indian, or something of the sort, but that's no excuse.'

The tight muscles in his face twitched. 'For God's sake, thousands of soldiers are still loyal to their regiments and to the Crown, and fighting on our side. Tens of thousands more are going about their duties as usual. No one knows what the end of this will be. Find out what the devil got into the man. Threats, bribery, drunk and lost his wits? Give some explanation.'

Narraway felt dismay turn to anger. It was bad enough that he was picked out to defend the indefensible; now Strafford required him to explain it as well.

'If Corporal Tallis has an explanation, sir, I shall offer it,' he replied in a hard, controlled voice. 'I cannot imagine one that will excuse his conduct, so it will be brief.'

'The explanation is not to excuse him, Lieutenant,' Strafford said acidly. 'It is to help the garrison here feel as if there is some sense in the world, some tiny thread of reason to hold on to, when everything they know has turned into chaos and half the people we loved are slaughtered like animals, and the nation on every side is in ruins.' A flush spread up his fair face, visible even in this wavering light. 'You are here to satisfy the law so that we do not appear to history to have betrayed ourselves and all we believe in, not to excuse the damned man! I know you are new here, but you must have at least that much sense!'

'Strafford . . .' Latimer said quietly, interrupting for the first time. 'We have given the lieutenant a thankless task, and he is quite aware of it. If he isn't now, he will be when he has looked at it a trifle more closely.' He turned to Narraway again. 'Lieutenant, we do not know where we shall be by the turn of the year, here or somewhere else, besieged or comparatively free. This matter must be dealt with before then. The women and children need a celebration, however meagre. We need hope, and we cannot have that without a quiet conscience. We cannot celebrate the birth of the Son of God, nor can we ask His help with confidence, if we do so with dishonour weighing us down. I expect you to conduct Tallis's defence in such a manner that we have no stain on our conduct to cripple us in the future. Do I make myself clear?'

Narraway took a deep breath and let it out slowly. 'Yes, sir,' he said as if he had some idea in his head how to do it. It was a lie, by implication, as he saluted and left the room. He had no idea whatever.

He walked away from the command building across the dry earth without any notion of where he was going. It was totally dark now, and the sky was burning with stars and a low, three-quarter moon. There was sufficient light to see the broken outline of the walls and the black billows of the tamarind trees, motionless in the still air. His feet made no sound on the dry earth.

He passed few other people, even on the road beyond the intrenchment. Sentries took no notice of him. In his uniform he passed unquestioned.

Half a mile away the vast Ganges River murmured and shifted in the moonlight, reflecting an almost unbroken surface, only streaked here and there where the current eddied.

The prisoner who had escaped and the guard he had so savagely murdered were both Sikhs. That in itself was not extraordinary. The Sikhs had been on either side during the mutiny. India was made up of many races and religions, languages and variations in culture from region to region. Petty wars and squabbles abounded.

John Tallis was British, but one of his grandparents had been Indian — Narraway had no idea from where, or even if they had been Hindu, Sikh, Jain, Muslim or something else. He

9

dreaded meeting the man: yet, as soon as he had any clarity in his mind as to how he should approach the subject, he must do it.

The crime had been monstrous and there could be no defence. The guard, Chuttur Singh, had been hacked to death. It had not been even a simple breaking of the neck, or cutting his throat, which, while gruesome, would at least have been quick. The massacre of the patrol was equally bloody, but it was, in a sense, part of war and so to be expected. But it would not have happened had the enemy not known exactly where to find them, and at what hour.

What had changed John Tallis from a first-class medical aide of compassion and loyalty into a man who could betray his own?

Narraway was walking slowly, but already he was on the beginning of the street that led into the battered and bedraggled town. In the distance he could see the spires of two of the churches against the skyline. Nearer him there were a couple of shops with their doors closed. There was hardly anyone around, just a glimpse of light visible here and there from a half-shuttered window, a sound of laughter, a woman singing, the smell of food. The air was chilling rapidly with the darkness. If he stood still he would become aware of the cold.

He started to walk again, smelling the dampness of the river as he came closer to it. The earth was softer under his feet.

What did Latimer really expect of him? He had implied that he required Narraway to find something that made sense of Tallis's act. People needed to understand. No one can fight chaos. Maybe unreason is the last and worst fear, the one against which we have no weapons?

Was Latimer, as the man in command, the one everybody looked towards, trying to create a belief in order, a reason to fight?

Narraway came through the last trees and stared across the surging water, away to the north-east where he knew Lucknow was, beyond the horizon. Exactly a month before Christmas, General Havelock had died outside the city, worn out, beaten and bereaved. Had he finally seen the consuming darkness of loss and panic, and been overwhelmed by it, unable to see hope?

How much morale is affected by the character of a leader? It was a lesson Narraway had been taught over and over again, both at school and, later, in his military training. An officer must know his tactics, must understand both his own men and his enemy, must be familiar with the terrain and with the weapons, must guard his supply lines, must gain all the intelligence of the enemy that he possibly can. Above all he must earn the trust and the love of his men. He must act decisively and with honour, knowing what he is fighting for and believing in its worth.

Latimer had to deal with John Tallis immediately, and in such a way that no one afterwards would look back on it with shame. They needed that for their own survival.

Victor Narraway had been chosen to bear the burden of defending a man totally indefensible. He was strategically and emotionally trapped, exactly as if he were besieged himself in the city of his own duty, and there was no escape, no relief column coming.

It was already late. There was no point in waiting any longer. The situation would not get better. He turned away from the sheet of light on the river and walked into the shadows again, making his way back towards the barracks and the makeshift prison where John Tallis was being kept until his trial, and inevitable sentence to death.

He must begin tonight.

★　★　★

The guards stood to attention outside the prison door. In the darkness it was hard to see their faces and their expressions appeared blank. They looked at Narraway with indifference. One of them held up an oil lamp. They were both young, but they had been in India long enough for their fair skins to be burned dark by the sun. They recognised the insignia of rank on Narraway's uniform.

'Yes, sir?' the taller of the two said with no flicker of interest.

'Lieutenant Narraway, to see the prisoner,' Narraway told him. He expected distaste, a forced civility. He saw nothing at all. Was the man genuinely impartial, or — after the siege — had he no feelings left?

'Yes, sir,' the man said obediently. 'You'll pardon me, but may I have your side-arm, sir? No weapons allowed in when you're with the prisoner.'

Narraway remembered with a chill that the prisoner who escaped had murdered the guard with his own weapon. He handed over his revolver without demur.

A moment later he was inside the cell with John Tallis, standing face to face. Tallis was tall, a little hunched over. He was naturally lean, but low rations and the exhaustion of first the long, burning summer under siege, and now imprisonment, had left him gaunt. He still wore his army uniform, but the trousers bagged on him. The tunic hung hollow over his chest and pulled a little crookedly at the shoulders. His thick, black hair was lank, and his blue eyes startling against the sun-weathered skin of his face. He might have been any age, but Narraway knew he was thirty.

Narraway introduced himself. 'I'm going to defend you at trial,' he explained. 'I need to talk to you because I have no idea what to say. I know your regimental history because it's a matter of record. Everyone agrees, you were one of the best medical orderlies they've ever known.'

He saw Tallis lift his chin a little and give a twisted, self-mocking smile. His teeth were white and perfect.

'That'll come in useful if I'm ever charged with incompetence,' he said, his voice cracking a little. 'Unfortunately it doesn't help now.'

Narraway struggled for something to ask that might offer any mitigation. What on earth did Latimer think he could do? There was no defence! He was going to be completely useless. No wonder Latimer did not give the task to any of the men who had served with him long and loyally.

'Tell me what happened,' Narraway said aloud. 'Exactly. Give me all the details you can remember. Go back as far as you need, to make some sense of it.'

Tallis looked incredulous. 'Sense? When did you get here? Yesterday? There isn't any sense. It's a colossal pile-up of one idiocy after another. Bullets greased with pig fat, cow fat. It's probably bloody mutton anyway! Nobody's listening to anyone. Half of them are just settling old scores, or shooting at anything that moves.'

'You must have had some reason for helping Dhuleep,' Narraway said desperately. 'Give me something, anything at all to say on your behalf.'

Tallis's eyes opened wider. A look of terror was naked in their blue depth for a moment, then he concealed it. He swallowed convulsively, his throat so tight he all but choked. 'I didn't do it,' he answered. 'And I haven't any idea who did.'

Narraway was totally at a loss. Tallis was not justifying himself, not making excuses, not blaming anyone else, just giving a sheer, blank denial.

'There was no one else who could have,' he said as calmly as he could manage. 'Everyone else's whereabouts are accounted for, one way or another.'

'Then someone is lying, or got it wrong,' Tallis answered. 'I did not kill Chuttur Singh, or let Dhuleep Singh go. You have to prove that.'

'I've got less than two days,' Narraway protested. 'Captain Busby's already been through it

14

all, and Major Strafford.'

'I didn't do it,' Tallis said simply. He gave a shrug of his bony shoulders. 'I'm a medical orderly. I only kill people by accident, never on purpose.'

Narraway was startled, angry; then suddenly he saw the black humour in Tallis's eyes. In that instant he felt a wave of compassion for the man's courage. In other circumstances, a thousand miles from here, he could have liked him. He licked his dry lips. 'Where were you when Chuttur Singh was murdered?' he asked.

Tallis thought for a moment. 'From when they say it must have happened, I was in the storeroom, alone. I was counting what we had, and what we could possibly get hold of if there were any kind of relief supplies come in, and what we could make for ourselves with things from the bazaar,' he replied. 'If I could prove it, I would have already. It's a pretty good mess in there. We've been making do for a long time. I'm just about out of inventions.'

'Did you not make lists of anything, notes of what to get?' Narraway struggled for any answer at all.

'Certainly,' Tallis replied, 'but I can't prove when I wrote them. Could have done it any time in the previous twenty-four hours. Believe me, I count those damn things in my sleep, hoping I've got it wrong, and there are more left than I thought. I sometimes even get up in the night and count them again, hoping they've got together and bred — like bedbugs.'

Narraway ignored the analogy. 'Did you know

15

Chuttur Singh?' he asked.

Tallis looked away, his voice thick with emotion. 'Yes. He was a good man. Silly sense of humour. Always coming up with crazy jokes that weren't funny. He made me laugh, just because he laughed.'

That sounded so normal to Narraway, and absurd that they should now be talking about murder and execution. It was a nightmare he must wake up from. He used to know how to do that, when he was a boy — make himself wake up. 'And Dhuleep?' he asked.

'Different altogether,' Tallis replied, watching Narraway closely. 'Quiet. Never knew what he was thinking. He used to recite poetry to himself. At least I think it was poetry. It could have been a string of curses, or a recipe for curry, for all I know. Or a letter to his grandmother.' He blinked. 'If they hang me, will you write a letter to my grandmother? Tell her I died bravely? Even if I don't?'

Narraway drew in his breath to remonstrate with him, tell him not to be flippant, or not to give up hope, but the words slipped through his mind and were all useless. They were going to hang Tallis in a couple of days, get the whole matter dealt with and out of mind before Christmas, for everybody's sake — everybody except Tallis, and his family back in England, proud of him.

'If it should prove necessary, and you give me an address, of course I will,' he said instead, as if it were the natural answer. But it was also of no help at all. Did that mean Tallis had accepted

16

that he would be found guilty and hanged?

Narraway could not give up so soon. Latimer was looking for more than surrender; he needed some answer that allowed hope, a spark of sanity in the weariness and the fear.

'Somebody killed the man, and you're the only one unaccounted for,' he pointed out sharply. 'Everyone else was busy, and in someone else's sight. Look, if you had a reason for killing him, if you know something about him, tell me.' He started to say that for Tallis's own sake he should explain it, then stopped abruptly. Whatever Tallis said, it would make no difference at all to his death. He would be hanged and they both knew it. To lie would be both a pointless and a squalid thing to do. It would break the spider-thin thread of connection between them that was his only chance.

He began again. 'The regiment needs to know. There's chaos and death all over the place, everywhere. We need at least to believe in ourselves.'

Tallis closed his bright blue eyes. 'My God, you're young! What — nineteen? This time last year you were sitting exams behind some neat, wooden school desk, waiting for a bell to ring and tell you time's up.'

'Twenty!' Narraway snapped, feeling the colour burn up his face. 'And I — ' He stopped short, stung by shame at the absurdity of thinking of himself. Tallis was facing trial for his life, and he had been offered nothing better than the most junior lieutenant to defend him.

Narraway lowered his voice and kept it steady.

17

'Please, for the sake of the regiment, the men you know and who've trusted you, help them to make sense of this. Give them a reason, whatever it was. Why did you want to rescue Dhuleep? What did you think he was going to do? If you didn't mean to betray the patrol, or get Chuttur killed, what went wrong? If someone is lying, who? And why?'

Tallis stared at him, started to speak, then stopped again.

'Are you protecting someone else?' Narraway asked sharply. 'Is this some debt of honour you owe?'

Tallis was completely stunned. No denial in words could have carried such complete conviction. 'Debt of honour?' he said incredulously, then he started to laugh, quietly, but with a jarring, hysterical note underneath it.

Narraway felt ridiculous, and painfully helpless. He had expected anger, despair, self-pity, but not this.

Then Tallis stopped laughing as suddenly as he had begun.

'I did not murder Chuttur Singh in a debt of honour,' he said quietly, almost mildly, as if the idea were no part of reality. 'I'm a medical orderly who just happens to be wearing a soldier's uniform. I save lives — any lives. I'd treat a sick dog, if I had one. My honour is to medicine.'

Narraway could think of nothing to say. He did not know even where to begin.

'For God's sake, man, think!' he said desperately. 'Who was friendly with Dhuleep?

Who might have owed him something, or sympathised with him? Is it possible anyone had a . . . a debt to cancel, or a feud with anyone on the patrol that was wiped out? If it wasn't you, then it has to have been someone else.'

Tallis's brilliant blue eyes opened wide. 'Is that why I'm supposed to have done it? Because I owed something to someone, or hated someone on the patrol? I'm a medical orderly. I don't even know who was on the damn patrol! I'm one of the few men in the station who never has time to gamble or run up any debts. Half our medical staff were killed in the siege, and it's not as if we can just promote up who's left.'

'Then think of anything you've heard, gossip, tales,' Narraway urged him. 'We've no time.'

'I've no time,' Tallis corrected him. 'The regiment needs it out of the way as quickly as can be made to look decent. I can't blame them for that. I suppose I would in their place.' He pulled his lips tight. 'Happy Christmas, Lieutenant.'

★　★　★

Narraway slept badly. Such dreams as he had were tangled and filled with a sense of hopelessness. He woke fighting against the sheets as if they were binding him, keeping him from escape. He was gasping for breath, in spite of the fact that there was nothing over his face.

Again and again he saw Tallis's eyes. Was he innocent? Could it be a monstrous mistake? Or could the authorities so desperately need to find

19

the traitor, and make everyone believe justice had been done, that actual justice was the price?

But what other answer could there be? It seemed that no one else had had the opportunity to kill Chuttur Singh, so by default it had to have been Tallis. But what reason had he? What was Narraway missing that would make sense of it?

He was so tired his head pounded and his eyes felt full of grit.

★ ★ ★

He rose early, washed, shaved and dressed before going to the mess and taking a brief breakfast. He liked the fruit they had in the summer — mangoes, bananas and guavas — but there were none left now. He acknowledged other officers but sat alone where he could avoid conversation. He needed to think.

Latimer had given him today in which to create some kind of defence for Tallis. An appeal for mercy was pointless. The only answer to a verdict of guilty was execution. Soldiers were killed all the time. Cawnpore was steeped in blood. Death was cheap. One more was barely even noticeable.

After he had eaten he went outside and walked along the dusty roadway. The low bungalow houses of the officers were ramshackle buildings now: three or four rooms set in extended areas that in better times would have been gardens. He did not hear the silent footsteps behind him and was only aware of Captain Busby when he spoke, almost at his elbow.

'Morning, Lieutenant,' Busby said briskly, not disguising the fact that he had obviously found him intentionally. 'Good idea to get away from the barracks a bit. Glad you thought of it.'

'Good morning, sir,' Narraway replied tersely, wondering what Busby wanted with him. He was not ready to discuss strategy yet, or accept any instruction, for that matter.

They came to a crossroads. Busby moved closer, obliging Narraway to accept the tacit guidance and turn along the wider road into the town.

The first building they passed was the library, looking dusty and deserted, its doors closed. There were two women standing on the steps with books in their hands, chatting to each other then glancing up the street towards tea rooms and the general direction of the bazaar.

A couple of men came down from the breakfast club on the opposite side and nodded, touching their hats courteously. They looked serious, avoiding anything more than the minimum acknowledgement of Busby and Narraway.

The billiard rooms were deserted this early in the day, as was the Freemasons' Lodge with its handsome entrance. Narraway had intended to go towards the river. He did not want the noise and the constant interruptions with pleas to buy this or that, but Busby was intent on conversation and he could not escape.

'Doesn't look the same as it used to,' Busby said ruefully as they passed the doors of the newsrooms. 'Everyone's trying, of course, but the memories of the siege are all over the place, and the fear it will happen again. Every place you look at makes you think of someone that's gone. Thank God it's Christmas soon. Remind us who we are, what we believe in.' He was talking quite casually, but his voice was edged with tension. He was a fraction taller than Narraway, and perhaps seven or eight years older. His fair skin was burned a red-brown by the Indian sun and he walked with a very slight limp, as if from an old wound. There was a thin scar on the side of his left cheek, hardly noticeable.

'Yes, sir,' Narraway agreed, as they passed the theatre where in better times the younger men had performed all kinds of music and comedies for the general entertainment. It was silent now. 'I've seen some of the children making garlands of coloured paper,' he added.

Busby smiled. 'We must protect them. They have a right to expect that of us. We bring them here, thousands of miles away from everything they knew and loved, and expect their total loyalty. We receive it, and sometimes I think we take it too lightly. We owe it to them, especially the wives of those killed on the patrol, to see this trial to a swift end.' He glanced at Narraway, and then back at the rutted road they were walking along. 'I hope you can see that.' He said it with a lift in his voice, as if it were, at least in part, a question.

He outranked Narraway, but in the matter of the trial of John Tallis, rank should mean nothing.

'As rapidly as justice allows, sir,' Narraway agreed.

'What witnesses do you propose to call?' Busby asked rather briskly.

'I don't know,' Narraway admitted. 'I only got the case yesterday evening, and I've never represented anyone on trial before.'

'For heaven's sake, you're an officer, man!' Busby said dismissively. 'I'm not a lawyer either. We're after the truth, not tricks of the law. A loyal Sikh officer has been cut to pieces and ten of our own men were ambushed out there on patrol.' He waved his arm in a general southerly direction. 'Nine of them are dead. We've got more widows, at least half a dozen more fatherless children. Tallis is responsible for that. We just need to do it legally, for our own sakes. Don't harrow up everyone's emotions and open old wounds by asking a lot of unnecessary questions.'

Narraway did not answer. There was no point in telling Busby that the colonel had asked for more than just tidying it away. He wanted to understand what had gone so terribly wrong.

They walked a few paces in silence. A man pushing a cart of vegetables veered and jolted over a hole ahead of them. Two women, probably officers' wives, from the cut of their clothes, passed on the opposite side, inclining their heads slightly.

'I'm not sure if you are the right man for this,' Busby went on, now staring straight ahead of himself. 'We might have been better with someone who'd actually been through the siege, and understood the suffering and the deeper issues.'

'I think Colonel Latimer chose me precisely because I haven't,' Narraway answered him. 'He wants it not only to be fair but, just as importantly, that it's seen to be. If I'd been here through the siege I'd have loyalties to certain men more than others, perhaps men to whom I owed my life. I might not favour them in any way, but people couldn't be sure of it.'

Busby walked in silence. They passed a small non-denominational church on the other side of the street. The post office was just ahead of them. They all looked battered, some scarred by shells that had exploded too close. One shop was darkened by fire, the stains spreading out like the shadow of a hand.

'I don't know who you're going to call,' Busby said suddenly. 'No one else could have done it, you know. Don't go trying to raise doubt as to the honour of decent men. Apart from the fact that you won't get Tallis off — and by God, neither should you — you certainly won't do yourself any favours. If you want to make a career in the army, you'll understand loyalty.' His voice took on a sudden, intense emotion. 'That's what it's all about — courage under fire, steadfastness, and loyalty. You're no damn use to man or beast if your own men don't know that, over hell or high water, they can trust you.'

He glanced sideways at Narraway, his eyes sharp. Then, after a moment's penetrating stare, he looked ahead again. 'I assume you know that already, and I don't have to tell you? Make a good job of this, and the whole regiment will respect you. Filthy responsibility, I know.'

'Yes, sir,' Narraway agreed, trying to put his words carefully. 'My aim is to defend Tallis so that no one afterwards — history, if you like — can say that he wasn't dealt with fairly. I hope that won't take time, and I sincerely hope that it won't necessitate my calling anyone as witness to an event that distresses them more than is unavoidable. But haste now may lead to dishonour, and to grief later on that will damage the regiment, and even the reputation of the Indian Army in the future.'

Busby stopped abruptly and swung around to face Narraway. 'I think I underestimated you, Lieutenant. You're going to be a damn nuisance, aren't you? But if you think you can teach me how to earn the regiment's loyalty you are profoundly mistaken. Which I will show you in a couple of days' time.'

'Yes, sir,' Narraway said with a brief flicker of satisfaction. 'I'm sure you will, sir, and with the utmost fairness. You can hardly fail to secure Tallis's conviction, considering the circumstances.'

'I don't just want to secure his conviction, damn it,' Busby said sharply. 'I want to get the matter over with, with the least pain to men and women who have suffered abominations you can't even begin to imagine.' He swivelled around and started to walk swiftly back towards the barracks, and the intrenchment where the army had been besieged. 'Come!' he commanded.

Narraway turned and followed him, catching up with an effort. He did not want to go to the intrenchment again. He knew what had happened there and could imagine the horror. It was a barren square of ground, a hundred yards or so in either direction, with two- or three-storey buildings along most of two sides. The rest was walled by simple earthworks, dug by spade and thrown up to less than the height of a man. During the eighteen days and nights of the incessant bombardment from Nana Sahib and his men, nine hundred people had lived there. Many had died of heat stroke, cholera or from their wounds.

Narraway still shuddered as he pictured the people huddled together, terrified, exhausted, trying to protect one another, waiting for a relief that never came. He could see the ghosts of them in his mind. He wanted to turn and walk away, but he could not ignore Busby, who was his senior officer. And perhaps even more than that, he did not want Busby to know how deeply affected he was.

He stood silently. If Busby had anything to say he would have to initiate it himself.

In the distance a dog barked, a woman called out a child's name. There was an echo of laughter, exactly as if everything were perfectly normal — sounds of life, like new green shoots after a forest fire.

'Don't let them down, Narraway,' Busby said at last. 'You owe them.'

Narraway wanted to say something brave, about justice being nothing to do with emotion or personal loyalties, but all the words that came to his mind sounded trite and they would only anger Busby. Worse than that, he would not mean them himself.

Busby was staring at him, waiting for his response.

'As I see it, sir,' Narraway began awkwardly, 'the most important thing is that when the mutiny's over and order is restored again, India knows that British justice is fair, sir.'

Busby shook his head, momentarily taken aback. He started to speak, and then changed his mind.

Narraway waited. He longed to leave this place, but he would not go until Busby did.

'I don't envy you,' Busby said at last. 'I suppose you have to make a show of it. Mind you do just enough.'

'I didn't choose it, sir,' Narraway answered.

'Nobody chooses their military duty, Lieutenant,' Busby said tartly. He stared across the intrenchment. 'These poor devils didn't choose to be here either. Just make as much of an effort as you have to so the hanging is fair.'

'Yes, sir,' Narraway answered automatically. He was not sure if he meant it.

Busby turned and began to walk back the way they had come, his shoulders squared, but there was no spring in his step, no vigour.

Narraway waited a few moments longer, then left also, feeling as if he were turning his back on the ghosts, in a way denying them.

He needed to think. At the moment all he had for a defence was to try to discredit the witnesses

Busby would call, and that was precisely what Busby had just warned him against. No one needed to tell him that attacking another man would earn him no friends. Most of them had already suffered deeply, lost both friends and, in some cases, wives they loved, seen horrors Narraway himself could only imagine. He had been in India a year but he was an outsider to Cawnpore, and no one would forget that.

If his father had not insisted that the army would make a better man of him than a few years at university, Narraway would now be huddling beside a fire in some lodgings in Cambridge, worrying about cramming for an exam, and looking forward to going home for Christmas. His greatest discomfort would be trifling cold, the greatest danger not doing well enough, getting lower marks than he should have.

He had not chosen this. He remembered his last evening at home before taking the train to Southampton, and then the ship on what had seemed an endless journey south around the Cape of Good Hope, into the Indian Ocean. There had been weeks cooped up, a tiny dot on a measureless expanse of water, everywhere he looked nothing but blue. They could have been the only men alive on the earth. Even the burning, blazing white stars in the sky above him changed, especially around the southern tip of Africa, before they started north again, and recrossed the equator.

For what? Some of the men he had learned to know on that ship were already dead in this savage mutiny — in so many cases, Indian against Indian. He had heard that there were only a little over twenty thousand Queen's troops in India, and of course far more East India Company men, with all their wives and children — as opposed to Indians numbering uncounted millions.

Without realising it, he was walking towards the river. Its swift, brown water was dangerous: full of creatures of sorts — and probably snakes as well — at least along the banks. But it still held a fascination for him: a sense of width and a freedom that the land did not.

Was that a log floating half-submerged in the water? Or a crocodile? If he watched that to see, what else would he miss? Crocodiles sometimes came out on to the banks. He had seen their teeth, like a double row of jagged nails, needle-sharp. They could take a man's leg off in a single movement. He did not believe the stories that they were not aggressive, and preferred to eat fish.

Was Narraway Tallis's best chance, or his worst? There was only one possible end for him — the gallows. The difference lay in whether it appeared that someone had fought for him, or not. Narraway himself was expendable. If everyone loathed him afterwards and he went down in history as the man who had tried to excuse Tallis, that was the price of a swift and unquestioned execution, and the matter laid to rest before Christmas.

And if John Tallis were innocent? Was that even possible?

The log in the river moved, and sank gracefully beneath the water, leaving a momentary wake behind it.

Crocodile.

The facts said that Tallis was the only one who could be guilty. And yet seeing his face again, recalling it as vividly as if it had been moments ago — the clear, burning blue eyes — doubts arose in Narraway's mind, irrational but undeniable doubts.

Then who could be guilty? Who was lying? He could not imagine that several men were all lying to save the man who had really murdered Chuttur Singh and let Dhuleep go, then to betray the patrol. And worse than that, they would then allow Tallis to be executed for it?

Narraway could not get rid of the feeling that Tallis trusted him. All sorts of arguments came into his mind as to why it was not trust so much as hope, or a brilliant piece of acting. Or perhaps — which was the easiest to understand — it was a denial to himself that he could have committed such a betrayal, a refusal to face the fact of his own guilt.

But looking at Tallis, that was not what Narraway had felt. He believed he had seen real, desperate hope, the kind a man clings to who has truth on his side.

How could Narraway even begin? If Tallis were innocent — and that was the only assumption he could work with — then either someone was intentionally lying, presumably in order to defend themselves, or they were badly mistaken. Check everything, that was the only workable possibility. It would at least provide him with his own facts. Stand where they had each said they had been, prove for himself that they had seen what they had said, time it all, go over the work they claimed to have done. Find the mistakes, the excuses, or the lies.

He turned and headed back through the trees towards the town.

The events of the mutiny were about a year old. It had begun in January, in Dum Dum. Almost every day since then there had been some new disaster, victory and then reversal, siege and relief, a new uprising somewhere else. How ridiculous to be trying one soldier for the death of one guard in the middle of Cawnpore while all over northern India tens of thousands of men shot and slashed and stabbed each other, men that a year ago they had trusted without hesitation.

He looked around at the sprawling houses of the officers with their verandas, their wide, scruffy gardens, the tamarind and mango trees, the lazy wind not stirring the leaves. In the summer the heat had been furnace-like, brutal. Now, at night, it was sometimes even cold.

He was not fighting with sword or rifle, although that would come soon enough. Scores of towns and cities were besieged or already fallen. This was only a respite.

In the meantime, as this day dwindled into nothing and disappeared, Narraway must prepare for the hopeless task of pretending to defend John Tallis, for which everyone would despise him, in spite of the fact that they knew

31

he had no choice. He was cast as the second villain in a charade.

He increased his pace a little. The only course he could think of was to speak with the witnesses Busby would be bound to call. That had to be the three men who answered the alarm and found Chuttur Singh dying on the floor in a pool of his own blood, and Dhuleep Singh gone.

He was walking past one of the rows of houses where various non-commissioned officers had their homes. They were all built of brick coated with white plaster in various degrees of shabbiness. Verandas ran around three sides of each one, a flight of half a dozen or so steps leading up to the door. They stood separately in their own arid two or three acres, as if space were no object at all.

Narraway knew what they were like inside. The main door led into a wide, comfortless sitting room, full of over-used furniture, looking rather as if salvaged from a second-hand sale, and intended only for temporary use, until something worthier could be found.

On either side would be smaller rooms, for beds, and probably one for a bath. The water for it, when needed, was left to cool outside in a row of huge porous red jars, so the officer's bath might be refreshing.

He looked back at the road and saw ahead of him a woman walking slowly. She had a small child in her arms and a large bundle of shopping carried in a string bag, its handles biting into her other shoulder. She was bent under the weight of it, and limping slightly, although from what he

32

could see of her slender figure, she was not many years older than he.

Narraway increased his pace and caught up with her.

'Ma'am!' he said more loudly than he had meant to.

She halted and turned slowly. Her face was gaunt, and there were smudges of dirt where the child's dusty fingers had touched her cheek, but her skin was smooth, blemishless.

'Yes?' she said without curiosity. There was anxiety in her eyes, a shadow not unlike fear.

'May I carry the bag for you?' he asked. 'I'm going the same way you are. Please?' he added. He smiled at her. 'My day has been fairly useless so far. I'd like to do something to make it better.'

She smiled at him, suddenly and radiantly. It took away all the weariness, and showed that she was indeed probably no more than thirty at the most, and pretty.

'Thank you, Lieutenant,' she accepted. She made a move to put the child down so she could unhook the bag and pass it to him, but he eased it off her shoulder and took it without her needing to. It startled him with its weight. No wonder she had moved so slowly. The strings of it must have hurt her.

They started to walk again, still fairly slowly.

'You are new here,' she observed, looking straight ahead of her. The child in her arms looked to be less than two, probably well able to walk, but not this far, or at the speed she would have chosen. It regarded him solemnly with long-lashed eyes of golden brown. Its hair was

33

curly, and long enough for Narraway to be uncertain if it was a boy or a girl.

'Does it show so much?' he asked, referring to her observation as to his newness here. 'Or do you know everybody?'

'Most of them,' she replied. 'Of course people come and go a lot, just at the moment.' She made a sad little grimace. 'But you look paler, as if you weren't here during the heat.' Then she blushed at her lack of tact in having made so personal an observation. 'I'm sorry.'

'No reason to apologise,' he replied. 'I suppose I stick out like a row of sore thumbs anyway.'

She laughed at the image of such a thing. 'Next time I see you in the parade ground, I shall think of a row of sore thumbs,' she said cheerfully. 'That will be a new insult for the sergeant major to think of. Except that I see you're a lieutenant. I don't suppose you do a lot of marching around to orders.'

'Not in the way you mean,' he replied. 'Although I feel rather a lot as if I'm marching round and round, to orders, and accomplishing nothing.'

She looked at him curiously. 'A lot of army life is like that. At least my husband always used to say so.'

He heard the past tense in her speech, and saw the moment of pain, the tightening of her arms around the child. There did not seem any help or meaning in saying anything, so he walked beside her in silence for twenty or thirty yards. Then a hideous thought occurred to him. Had her husband been one of the soldiers on the patrol

34

that Dhuleep Singh's betrayal had killed? Suddenly, intensely, he realised that he could not afford to know the answer. He could not tell her who he was, and he was ashamed of that. It was a new and much harder bite into the soft flesh of his self-belief. How horribly lonely he was going to be after he had stood up to defend John Tallis, never mind that he had been ordered to, and that they could not hang him until justice had been formally satisfied.

He had been trying to frame a few questions to ask her about Tallis, anything to learn a little background. Now the words froze on his tongue. The strings of the bag were cutting into his hands. He wondered what was inside it. No doubt fruit, vegetables, rice, food for herself and the child. Would she marry again one day, and have more children, or was this one going to grow up alone?

He wanted to speak with her. It seemed cold to walk side by side and say nothing, but consciousness of what the next couple of days would bring, and how differently she would see him, kept him silent. How long would it take him to live it down? The man who tried to defend John Tallis! Is that who he would remain to the people here?

She stopped at a gateway outside a house exactly like all the others, at least from the outside.

'Thank you,' she said with a shy smile. She bent and put the child down. It stood uncertainly on its feet before gaining its balance, then sitting down suddenly.

'I'll carry the bag as far as the step for you,' Narraway replied. 'Then you can carry him.' He gestured towards the child, who was making an unsuccessful attempt to stand up again.

'Her,' she corrected him. 'Thank you.' She bent and picked the child up again.

Narraway followed her up the path. They were still several yards short of the veranda steps when the front door burst open and a boy of about five came running out, a streamer of bright red paper in his hand.

'Mamma!' he shouted with triumph. 'I made three chains! All colours. And Helena made one too. It's not as good as mine, but I showed her how.'

'That's wonderful,' she smiled back at him. He had curly brown hair like hers, but huge dark eyes that must have come from his father. 'Helena?' she called out. 'David said you made a chain too. Come and show me.'

A girl of perhaps three stood inside the door, looking at Narraway warily.

'Come on!' her mother encouraged her.

Slowly she came across the veranda and took the steps, one down, standing on it, then the next down. She had a bright blue paper chain trailing behind her. She reached the bottom and joined her brother. She held the chain out to her mother, but her eyes were on Narraway all the time, curious but guarded.

He looked at the chain. 'It's beautiful,' he told her solemnly. 'Did you really make it yourself?'

She nodded.

'Then you are very clever,' he said.

Slowly, shyly, she smiled at him, showing white baby teeth.

'It's for Christmas,' the boy explained. 'To put up in the house.'

'It will be lovely,' he answered.

'Do you have Christmas?' Helena asked him.

'Course he does, silly!' her brother shook his head at her ignorance. 'Everybody has Christmas!' He looked at Narraway. 'She's only three. She doesn't know,' he explained.

Helena held out the bright blue chain. 'You can have it, if you like,' she offered.

He drew in breath to refuse, politely, but saw the smile again, and the hope. He glanced momentarily at the woman, uncertain what to do.

'Take it.' Her lips formed the words silently.

Narraway bent down a little to reach the chain and touched it. It was smooth and bright, the paper stuck together a trifle crookedly.

'Are you sure?' he asked. 'It's very beautiful. Don't you want to keep it?'

She shook her head, still holding it out to him.

'Thank you very much indeed.' He took it gently, in case she changed her mind at the last moment and clung on to it. 'I shall put it up in my house, near where I sit, so I can see it all the time.' She let it go and it fell loose in his hands.

The woman picked up the baby and carried her up to the top of the veranda steps, and Narraway handed the bag up, then waited as they all went inside, the two older children still watching him as he turned and walked down the path again, holding the blue paper chain in his hand.

* ★ ★

The prison where Dhuleep Singh had been held
faced on to a large, open yard with buildings on
three sides, and an open dogleg way out, which
was where most of the observation had taken
place. Men had been working at various jobs of
maintenance and repair, the sort of routine tasks
that occupied most of a soldier's day when not in
battle or marching from one place to another.
They were tedious, but better than standing idle.
It was easy to imagine leaving such a post, and
then having to be a little imaginative with the
truth in order to cover your absence.

Narraway stood in one place after another,
checking the angles of sight, the possibilities of
error or invention. Could any man have been so
absorbed in his work as not to notice someone
else pass by him? He did not believe it.

Had anyone left his stated position, and then
had to cover his absence? It seemed like the only
answer. Proving it would be almost impossible.
Even the attempt would earn him enemies.

★ ★ ★

He began his questioning with Grant. He was
the first man to reach the prison after Chuttur
Singh had raised the alarm. He was not yet on
duty, having been on guard most of the night.
Narraway went to see Grant, feeling mildly guilty
for wakening the man when he must have been
tired, but time left him no alternative.

Narraway went in through the gate, past some

ponies picketed near a magnificent mango tree. He walked briskly to the veranda, up the steps and knocked on the door. He knocked a second time, not really expecting an answer, then pushed it open and went in.

'Corporal Grant!' he called clearly.

There was silence.

Rather than call again he crossed the sitting room. There was a large, rickety table in the centre with a half-bottle of brandy on it, four empty soda water bottles, and a corkscrew. Used glasses sat where four card players had obviously been the previous evening. There was also a box of cigars, a few odd magazines, a rather ornate ink-stand, a bundle of letters and a revolver.

The rest of the furniture he ignored, going past more chairs, a battered Japanese cabinet, a corner stand with assorted hog spears, buggy whips and a shotgun. He did glance at the various pictures hung from nails in the wall, hoping they might give him some idea as to Grant's origins and character. There was a school photograph. There was also a painting of a soldier and a woman in clothes of perhaps twenty or twenty-five years ago, judging from the style of the woman's hair and the line of as much of her dress as he could see. They were probably Grant's parents. When he saw the man he might be able to judge.

'Corporal Grant!' he called again, more loudly. He did not want to intrude into the bedroom. It would be ill-mannered. He would not appreciate a senior officer doing the same to him. Also he wished to make an ally of the man rather than an

39

enemy, at least to begin with. 'Corporal Grant!' he repeated.

There was a stirring from the room beyond, then the sound of feet on the floor and a rustle of fabric. A moment later Grant appeared in the doorway, tousle-haired, still half asleep. His trousers had been hastily pulled on, and his tunic was not yet fastened.

'Yes, sir. I am Grant,' he said.

'Sorry to disturb you,' Narraway began, having introduced himself. 'I wouldn't waken you now, except that I have only today to speak to everyone about the Tallis case. I've been detailed to defend him. Since you were the first on the scene, I should begin with you.'

Grant blinked. He was a good-looking young man, perhaps four or five years older than Narraway, with a slight country burr to his voice. Narraway placed his accent as Cambridgeshire, or a little further north. His hair was brown with a touch of auburn, and his skin burned by at least one Indian summer.

'Oh,' Grant sighed. 'I see. Well, I can't tell you anything further than I've already told Captain Busby. Sorry.'

'Finish dressing.' Narraway made it more a suggestion than an order. 'I'll make us tea.'

Grant gestured towards the third room. 'Kitchen's there. There are servants somewhere. Probably left me to sleep. I hate having them fussing around when I'm . . . ' He did not bother to finish the sentence. Narraway already knew he had woken him, and they both understood that this conversation was unavoidable.

Ten minutes later they sat in the central room. It had been hastily tidied, and there was tea in front of them on the table. Grant was in full uniform and freshly shaved. He still looked tired and there were dark smudges around his eyes. He seemed nervous, but Narraway attributed that to the stress of remembering a shocking experience and having to recount it in circumstances that would end in the execution of a man he had possibly known quite well, and certainly trusted.

'I don't know what I can tell you that makes any difference,' Grant said again.

'Just tell me what happened,' Narraway replied. 'If I know what you're going to say to Captain Busby, at least I have the chance to prepare for it.'

Grant shook his head. 'It won't make any difference,' he said unhappily. 'I don't know what the devil got into Tallis. I always thought he was a decent chap. In fact I liked him. Everyone did. Well . . . one or two of the officers thought his sense of humour was a bit off.' He looked up at Narraway quickly. 'They just didn't understand. When you deal with illness and injuries every day, if you don't laugh sometimes, even at crazy things, you go mad.'

'You been out here long?' Narraway asked, looking at Grant curiously, wondering what his experience had been that he spoke with such feeling.

'Couple of years,' Grant replied. 'I was in the Crimea before that.'

Narraway winced. The disasters of that war,

the fatal mistakes were legend already. 'Bala-clava?' he asked before he thought of the possible inappropriateness of the question in the present circumstances.

Grant pulled a wry face. 'Thank God for Colin Campbell,' he said briefly.

Narraway was impressed, in spite of himself. 'Were you there with him?'

Grant straightened in his seat a fraction, some of his weariness disappearing. That was an answer in itself. 'Yes. Another damn stupid war we got into by accident because we didn't look where the hell we were going!' He rubbed his hand over his brow, pushing the heavy hair back. 'Sorry. There are times when I'd put the whole damn government on horseback and order them to charge the enemy guns — with bullets coated in pig grease! Mixed metaphor. Sorry. I lost friends in that too.'

Narraway sat silent, thinking of all the young men who had died needlessly because someone didn't know, or didn't think what they were doing. Rivers of loss, every one of them somebody's son, somebody's friend.

Grant rubbed his hands over his face and drew in a long breath, letting it out in a sigh. 'Perhaps Tallis did go mad, poor bastard. I hate this more than facing the enemy in the field. But I can only tell you what I know.'

Narraway jerked himself back to the present.

'That's all I want,' he said quietly. It seemed odd, in this silent, rather shabby house, sitting over cups of tea, talking about betrayal and murder conversationally, but with hands that trembled, and voices that every now and then rasped in the throat. 'You heard the prison alarm,' he prompted. 'Where were you?'

'About a hundred yards away, in one of the outbuildings,' Grant replied. 'I was checking munition stores. I dropped what I was doing and went outside — '

'Did you see anyone else?' Narraway interrupted.

'Not ahead of me, and I didn't look behind. It's sort of cluttered there . . . sheds, outhouses, that sort of thing. There was a pony and cart off to the left. I just noticed it out of the corner of my eye as I ran to the prison.'

'Anybody else moving? Running?' Narraway asked.

'No. I must have been the nearest person that heard it.'

'When you got to the prison block, the outside door was open?'

'No. It's makeshift. The real prison was too badly shelled. This does pretty well because it was a magazine of some sort. Not hard to make a couple of cells, and the whole thing locks only from the outside. Ideal, really. Escape-proof, without help.'

'Any other prisoners?'

'None except Dhuleep.' Grant looked down at his lean, sunburned hands on the table. 'Before the mutiny there would be the occasional insubordination, drunken fights and things, maybe even a theft or two. Since the siege and the massacre no one steps out of line. Those of us left are . . . close.' He looked up, hoping

Narraway would understand without the need for explanation.

Narraway nodded. 'What had Dhuleep done?'

'Dereliction of duty. Off his guard post at night. I thought he'd just fallen asleep, or something like that. We're all tired, a bit jumpy,' he sighed. 'Of course he could have gone anywhere.'

'Most likely trying to find information about the patrol,' Narraway replied.

Grant looked down at the table again. 'Yes — I suppose so. Looks like it now, doesn't it?'

'How did you get in?'

'It's easy enough from the outside. The key's there.'

'What did you find when you got in?'

Grant's face tightened, his eyes bleak. 'The cell door was open. There was no one inside, just Dhuleep's bedding on the floor and a plate of food, spilled . . . and blood. Lots of it. Chuttur Singh was on the floor in the main room outside, lying near the door. He must have used his last ounce of strength to reach up and pull the alarm. There was a trail of blood from the cell across the floor where he'd crawled. He was in a terrible state, his uniform slashed half to pieces, scarlet with his own blood. His face was grey, what I could see of it. He could hardly move.' He stopped speaking for several seconds, emotion choking him at the memory.

Narraway waited.

A clock ticked on the mantelpiece. Somewhere outside a dog barked and a child shouted out, its voice innocent, happy.

'He was dying,' Grant went on with an effort. 'He told me Dhuleep had escaped and to go after him. He had to be stopped because he knew about the route of the patrol. I wanted to stay and help him. He was . . . there was blood everywhere!'

He looked up at Narraway, guilt agonised in his face. 'I should have stayed,' he said hoarsely. 'I left him and went after Dhuleep. I — I was desperate that he didn't get away, because of what Chuttur said about the patrol.'

'How long had he been in the cell?' Narraway asked.

'A day or two, I think,' Grant replied.

'So they didn't know he had this information, or they would have changed the patrol route, or time, or something?' Narraway insisted.

'Can't have,' Grant agreed miserably. 'But the patrol was ambushed. I know that for a fact.'

'How?'

'Tierney told me.'

'Tierney?'

'The one man from the patrol who lived, although he's in a bad way. He said they were taken totally by surprise and pretty well massacred. That's what letting Dhuleep go did. That's why they'll hang Tallis.' His voice cracked. 'God, it was a mess. No one else survived. Not that Tallis doesn't deserve it for what he did to poor Chuttur Singh. Regardless of what happened to the patrol, no one should die lying on the floor, alone. I shouldn't have left him.' Grant stared into the distance, perhaps into a place inside his head rather than beyond the walls of the small, shabby house. 'We didn't even get bloody Dhuleep, anyway!'

'Did you find any trail of him?' Narraway asked, although he could not think what difference it would have made in the end.

'Not then. I suppose we thought we were on his heels and we'd catch up with him if we went fast enough. Damn lot of use that was.' He sank into a silent misery, sitting slumped in the chair, his tea ignored.

'And the others arrived soon after you? Attwood and Peterson?' Narraway continued.

'Yes.'

'How long were you alone before they came?' Narraway asked.

Grant chewed on his lip. 'About half a minute, maybe more, maybe less.'

'Tell me what you did again, exactly?'

'I went to Chuttur Singh.' Grant was concentrating intensely, his mind back in those first awful moments. 'I . . . I saw all the blood and I knew he was fatally wounded. I just wanted to . . . I don't know. To say 'save him' is ridiculous. There was so much blood on his clothes, on the floor, it was clear he was beyond help. I suppose you don't think! You just . . . ' He stopped. His face was ashen.

Narraway tried to keep the image from forming in his own mind, and failed. 'You went to Chuttur Singh on the floor, and realised he was past help. Then what?'

'He said . . . 'Dhuleep's gone,' I think. Something about someone else coming in, took him by surprise. Let Dhuleep out. He was

46

mumbling, choking. I remember he said 'gone'. And then, 'Get him, he knows the patrol.' The man must have just gone that moment, however long it took Chuttur to crawl from the cell to the alarm.' Grant was sweating, as if in his imagination he had made that desperate crawl himself.

'Then what?' Narraway asked.

'Then I looked into the cell, and he was right . . . of course. Dhuleep was gone. There was nothing there except blood, and the heap of bedding, blood on that too. That was when Attwood and Peterson came.'

'You told them what had happened?' Narraway pressed him.

'I told them that Dhuleep knew about the patrol and we had to catch him. One of them — I don't remember which one — kneeled to see if he could help Chuttur, then we all went outside to hunt Dhuleep.'

'Did you go together or split up?' Narraway was still clinging to the hope that one of them might have seen someone else, anyone not where they had said they were.

Grant's voice took on a weariness. 'We started within sight of each other, then as we saw no sign of him, we split up. I went west. I think Attwood went south and Peterson down to the river, I'm not sure.'

'Did you draw others into the search? Ask people? Send anyone else out?' Narraway pressured.

'Yes, of course. Anyone we spoke to.'

'Did you find any sign of him?' Narraway went

47

on. 'What were you looking for anyway? Footprints? How would you recognise his? Anyone who'd seen him? Who else was around? Soldiers, women and children, civilians? Who could have seen him? Surely someone must, with the knowledge of hindsight?'

'Of course,' Grant agreed with a twisted smile. 'With hindsight! A Sikh soldier in uniform. Not remarkable on any military station in Northern India. No one knew it was Dhuleep. They probably didn't give him a second look.'

'He'd just slashed a man to death,' Narraway pointed out. 'Those long, curved swords they carry are lethal! You said there was blood everywhere. Poor Chuttur bled to death. Dhuleep wouldn't have escaped without a mark on him. His trousers might have kept out of it, being draped and tight at the ankles, as they are, and if they were dark or striped, you might not have noticed. But his tunic would be light, and they're loose and long-skirted.' He waited expectantly, watching Grant's face.

'Perhaps he took it off?' Grant replied after a moment or two. 'He'd have had to. You're right, there must have been blood on it. But he did get away, and it doesn't matter now. He'll be miles from here. God knows where. I certainly don't.'

'You said you didn't find any trace of him then.' Narraway was not ready to give up. 'Did you later?'

'Yes.' There was no light of satisfaction in Grant's face. 'There was blood, just splashes here and there. And stains against a wall, and a doorpost. Didn't help. I'd like to think some of it

48

was his, but I don't know whether Chuttur even got a blow in or not.'

He lowered his eyes, his mouth pulled tight. 'I'm sorry. I liked Tallis. He seemed to be one of the best, but if he engineered Dhuleep's escape then I'll be happy to see him hanged. I don't have to do anything but tell the truth for that. Someone came in from the outside. Had to. No other way. That person must have struck Chuttur, stunned him at least, and then let Dhuleep out, and maybe gone with him, leaving Chuttur to die.'

'You can't open that door except from the outside?' Narraway asked again.

'No. Didn't I say that?' Grant bit his lip. 'When Dhuleep went Chuttur couldn't even get out himself. Just raise the alarm, poor devil. You can't save Tallis, and you shouldn't.' He faced Narraway squarely. There was sadness in his eyes, but no doubt at all.

★   ★   ★

Narraway found Attwood, the second soldier to arrive at the prison, working in the magazine. He had to ask the sergeant for permission to release him for as long as Narraway required him. It was given grudgingly, and Narraway and Attwood stood in the shadow of the magazine's huge walls to talk. Narraway could not help wondering why General Wheeler had not chosen this for his intrenchment, rather than the miserable earthworks that he had.

Attwood was in his late twenties, a career

49

soldier with a scar down one cheek and a finger missing on his left hand. He was short and solid, barrel-chested, and had a vigorous Yorkshire accent. He regarded Narraway, who was from the south of England, with good-natured contempt.

'Nothing to help you, sir,' he said briskly. 'Heard the alarm. Ran to the prison. Got in straight behind Grant. Found the poor lad kneeling on the floor with Chuttur Singh, the prison guard. Decent feller. Get a loyal Sikh and you've got a damned good man. Best soldiers on earth, that lot, them and the Gurkhas. Bad and they're the very devil.'

'And Dhuleep Singh?' Narraway asked.

Attwood gave him a hard stare. 'Gone, o' course. 'E's not going to hang around, once the door's open, is 'e? Know you've got to put up some kind of a defence fer Tallis. It's the law, or we can't 'ang the bastard. But you're on a fool's errand. Not that we're short on fools around here,' he added grimly.

Narraway's temper flared. 'Anybody particular in mind, Sergeant?' he said sharply.

'Whatever damn fool put grease on the cartridges in Dum Dum, sir. Any idiot who'd served with Indians could've seen that one coming. Offend every last bleedin' one of them in one go!' He shook his head. 'Don't tell me it was some genius who actually wanted this bleedin' chaos from Delhi to breakfast time!'

Narraway felt a sharp recollection of what Grant had said about ignorance, but he could not afford to agree with Attwood, at least not openly.

50

'Fool's errand or not,' he replied, 'I have to do the best I can.'

Attwood grinned, showing a broken front tooth. 'Don't make a mess of it — sir,' he said cheerfully. The 'sir' was definitely ironic. 'We don't want to have to do it all again, so as we can 'ang 'im with a clear conscience. Honour of the regiment that you fail nobly. Sir.' In his own mind, and probably that of most soldiers, his three chevrons were worth more than the one pip on Narraway's shoulder. 'But you'll fail, either way. No question to it,' he added.

'Then help me to do it as nobly as possible,' Narraway snapped. 'When you were inside, what did you see, apart from Grant on the floor beside the dying guard?'

'No one else, sir,' Attwood answered dutifully. 'I looked into the cell where Dhuleep had been. No one there, just blood-stained bedding on the floor.'

'Lot of blood?'

'Quite a bit. As if there'd been a bit of a struggle, like Dhuleep slashing at Chuttur, one man armed with one o' them long Sikh swords — edges like a razor, they 'ave — the other one trying to defend 'imself and not making much of it. Bloody murder, it was. Hardly a battle at all. Thank Tallis for that. Must 'ave caught Chuttur a hell of a whack before 'e ever let Dhuleep out. Damn coward, if you ask me — sir.'

Narraway kept his temper with difficulty. It was not that he objected to what Attwood was saying, or to his contempt. He was angry with his own helplessness, and a degree of frustration

51

inside him because he resented the fact that Tallis had made Narraway like him, even made him believe, for a moment, in the possibility of his innocence.

'Did you hear what Chuttur Singh said to Grant?' he asked aloud.

'Don't remember the words exact, but 'e said that someone 'ad come in an' caught 'im by surprise. Didn't say 'oo, of course. Maybe 'e didn't even see. Poor devil was dying when we got there. Cut 'im to bits, that bastard did.' Attwood's face was bleak with anger and grief. He was a battle-seasoned soldier, but he was not immune to pain, or the loss of a fellow, even after the hundreds of deaths he knew of, and the whole brutal savagery of war.

'Couldn't 'elp 'im,' he went on. 'Told us to go after the prisoner. Said 'e knew the patrol's route, an' we 'ad to get 'im. We didn't, but by God, we tried.' He clamped his mouth shut and glared at Narraway out of tear-filled blue eyes, defying him to offer pity.

'Yes, Sergeant, I know that,' Narraway agreed quietly. 'Corporal Grant said you found traces of blood, and boot prints. Although I suppose they could have been anyone's. Nobody saw him, is that right?'

'Nobody that's saying so,' Attwood agreed.

'He must have had blood on him,' Narraway pointed out.

'To some people, one Sikh soldier looks like another,' Attwood said drily. 'Other folks are scared, keeping their eyes shut to what they don't want to see. Everybody's frightened and sick and too tired to see where they're going, half the time, never mind tell one Sikh from another. Lost too many people, sir. Too many women and children. Bloody barbarians. What kind o' people kill women an' children, I ask you?' He blinked, glaring at Narraway. 'Don't you string this thing out, sir. We need to finish it. Get it all squared away before Christmas. Remember 'oo we are, and why we're 'ere. Get me?'

'Yes, Sergeant, I do,' Narraway answered him. 'But it'll never be over if we don't do it properly.'

'Then do it properly — sir,' Attwood said abruptly. 'Now if you'll excuse me, I'll be getting back to my duty.' He saluted and, without waiting for Narraway's permission, he turned on his heel and marched back up towards the magazine.

★ ★ ★

Narraway found Peterson, the third man to arrive at the prison, sitting at ease under a tamarind tree. He was off duty for another hour or so, and was smoking a cigar alone, staring into the distance. He was a private soldier of two or three years' experience. When Narraway stopped in front of him and asked his name, he scrambled to his feet and saluted.

'Yes, sir,' he said obediently, stubbing the cigar out with reluctance.

'At ease, Private Peterson,' Narraway replied. 'I don't think I'll take up much of your time.' He looked at the dry grass the man had been sitting on and decided it looked comfortable enough.

He sat down gingerly and waited until Peterson did also.

'Tell me about the escape of Dhuleep Singh,' Narraway said.

Peterson looked at him with as much distaste as he dared show. 'You the officer who's going to defend Tallis?'

'Someone has to,' Narraway replied.

'You're new here, aren't you?' He added 'sir' after a moment's hesitation. It was not outrightly rude, but bordering on it.

'I've been in India nearly a year,' Narraway replied. 'I've only been in Cawnpore for a couple of weeks. Why? Is there something I should know?'

Peterson kept his expression as bland as he could. 'Thought so. You wouldn't defend Tallis if you'd been here any longer.'

'Why not? Don't you think he should be tried?'

Peterson remained silent.

'Rather we just hang him regardless?' Narraway asked. 'You're right, I haven't been here very long, not long enough to realise we'd sunk that far, anyway. Is there anybody else we should hang, while we're about it?'

Peterson flushed. 'No, sir. I just meant . . . I don't know how you can defend the man, that's all. The whole patrol was wiped out — all but Tierney, and he'll likely not make it. That's all down to Tallis, because if Dhuleep hadn't escaped, that ambush wouldn't have happened. If they'd been attacked out in the open it would've been a fair fight.'

'There's nothing fair about war, Private Peterson. I thought you would have known that, after three years' experience. But trials are supposed to be fair. That's the whole point of them. Justice, not revenge. We're meant to be above just hanging a man because we think he might have done something we don't like.'

Peterson swivelled around to face Narraway, his eyes blazing. 'Something we don't like?' He all but choked on the words. 'He slashed Chuttur Singh to death and let Dhuleep out to betray the patrol so they were ambushed and butchered. I think 'don't like' is a bit pale — sir!'

'Yes, it is,' Narraway agreed. 'And after we are satisfied that he is the one who is responsible, we'll hang him from the strongest branch, and leave him there to swing. But after — not before.'

'He's the only one who could have,' Peterson responded. 'Captain Busby questioned everyone. There's no one else it could be.'

'Then we'll have no problem proving that at trial,' Narraway said, surprised that he was still reluctant to give up all hope of any other answer. 'Tell me what happened when you got to the prison after the alarm went off.'

Peterson said essentially the same thing as Grant and Attwood had said. He chose slightly different words, more from his own vernacular, but the facts and emotions were the same. When he had finished, he kept his eyes fixed on the middle distance where two young women were walking with children by their sides. Narraway thought of the woman he had met earlier, and the children with their coloured paper chains, Helena's smile.

'We need this finished,' Peterson said quietly. He took a long breath and let it out slowly. He was not looking at Narraway, and yet he was very clearly speaking to him, his voice low and urgent. 'Everything we thought we knew for certain has got blown away. People we trusted turned round and killed us, all over the place. Even women and children. But Christmas is Christmas, any place. We've got to remember who we are. What things are like at home. What we believe in, if you . . . ' finally he turned and faced Narraway, meeting his eyes, ' . . . if you get what I mean, sir?'

'I get exactly what you mean, Private Peterson,' Narraway said with an upsurge of emotion that took him by surprise. Peterson had appeared so ordinary, even tongue-tied, and yet he had explained the heart of what was needed better than any of the officers. 'I'll do the best I can.' He said it as if it were an oath, then he stood up, and Peterson scrambled to his feet to salute him.

★ ★ ★

Finally Narraway went to the hospital to see the surgeon.

Perhaps the only point in speaking with Rawlins was to be aware of what Busby might draw from him, although even that was pointless. He could change nothing, nor even guard against it. He was going through the motions, because he had been ordered to. He wished he could forget Tallis's face, his eyes.

He went into the hospital building and walked along its almost deserted corridors, passing a few orderlies, a couple of soldiers with bandaged wounds, one on crutches. He asked for Rawlins and was directed onwards. The place smelled of blood, bodily waste, lye and vinegar. His stomach clenched at it, and he wished he could hold his breath. How many men — and women — had bled to death here, or died of disease?

He found Rawlins busy stitching a surface wound in a man's leg. Narraway had to wait until he had finished and could give his attention to a matter that for him was far from urgent.

He had a small office where he invited Narraway to sit down, waving him towards a rickety chair. He perched on the end of the table himself. Rawlins was a little more than average height, broad-shouldered, perhaps in his forties. His fair hair showed streaks of grey only as the light caught it. His skin was deeply burned by many years in the Indian sun. He was a handsome man, far more obviously English-looking than Narraway himself, but Narraway had heard that he had an Indian wife.

'Thought you'd be coming,' Rawlins observed. 'But there's nothing I can say that'll help you. Wish there were. I liked Tallis. He was a bit of a clown at times, but he was a damn good orderly. Would have made a good doctor, given the chance. Saved a few men's lives with nerve and quick thinking.' His face was suddenly bleak. 'Don't know what the devil happened to him.

About the best thing you can do for him is not give him false hope. There's only one way it can end.'

'He says he didn't do it,' Narraway replied. 'The facts say he must have, and yet I find myself hard put not to believe him. Or at least not to think that he believes himself. Why would he do it?'

Rawlins shrugged. 'God knows. Why would anyone, except somebody who agrees with the mutineers? But if you really do, why the hell not join them? Staying here he has a good chance of being killed anyway. It isn't going to get better in the near future. What a bloody mess. The last thing we need is to lose a really good medical orderly. Ask your questions. It's a waste of time, but I assume you have to go through the motions.'

'I don't know what else to do,' Narraway admitted. 'There isn't any defence for such a thing.' He wanted to tell Rawlins how helpless he felt, and how totally confused by Tallis, but he despised complainers. 'Busby's bound to ask you about Chuttur Singh. The way Grant describes it, he was struck on the head, probably dazed. Tallis took his sword and when he had let Dhuleep out of his cell, Dhuleep hacked Chuttur to death. Does that fit in with the medical evidence?'

'Seems to,' Rawlins replied, his face puckered with regret. 'I can't see anything else possible, honestly. Certainly Chuttur had the exact injuries you describe. The Court will draw the obvious conclusion. Someone got in from the outside. Someone struck Chuttur, taking him by surprise, or he'd have defended himself. He was not armed, and Dhuleep was locked in his cell. There had to be a third man. According to everyone Busby's questioned, there was no one else except Tallis. Everyone else can account for themselves. It's hard to believe, and I wish to hell it were different, but it isn't. Pointless trying to deal with anything except reality. Sorry.'

'Any idea if Dhuleep was injured as well?' Narraway asked.

'Apparently he left blood here and there where he stopped as he escaped, but not much,' Rawlins answered. 'Smudges, smears on a wall, a couple of footprints edged with blood. If he was hurt at all, and it wasn't just poor Chuttur's blood he'd carried on his clothes, then he wasn't hurt badly, unfortunately. I'd like to think the swine was dead, lying out there in the scrub somewhere, or on one of those stony riverbeds being picked apart by the carrion birds. But he got as far as the rebels, because he told them where to ambush the patrol.'

His face was tight with a sudden wave of emotion. If someone had brought the bodies back, Rawlins would need to have seen them, perhaps identified them before burial. And he would have treated the man who came in alive but died from his injuries, and Tierney, the one survivor. Narraway would very much rather be a soldier than an army surgeon. Even trying to defend Tallis was better than Rawlins' job.

'I don't suppose it matters anyway,' he agreed. 'As you say, the facts allow only one explanation.

I can't think of any way to twist it to anything else. How is Tierney doing? Will he make it?'

'Could do,' Rawlins replied. 'Lost a leg. Wish I could have saved it, but it was shattered. You can see him if you want to, but I doubt he can tell you anything. No question they were betrayed by Dhuleep, not that it makes any difference to your case either way. I wouldn't waste your time, and the Court's, even raising that question.'

'I'll see him, if he's up to it.' Narraway stood up. 'I don't want to . . . upset him . . . '

Rawlins straightened to his feet. 'He might be glad of someone to talk to. He's still in a bad way, just lying there alone most of the time. We do what we can for the pain, but he's not a fool. He knows we're still all clinging on by our fingernails, as it were. We could all be dead in a few months, if we don't turn this tide. The news is bad, isn't it?'

'Yes,' Narraway confessed. 'Far as I know. But we've got Campbell. He could turn the tide, by Christmas. Remember the Crimea, Balaclava?'

Rawlins grinned lopsidedly. 'The Heavy Brigade: 'Here we stand, here we die.'' He quoted Campbell's famous exhortation to his men. 'Not exactly what I had in mind.'

'He won,' Narraway pointed out.

'Yes, why shouldn't the tide turn?' Rawlins agreed. 'I'll take you to see Tierney, if he's awake. That's for his sake, not yours. He can't tell you a damn thing that'll be any use to you. This way.'

Rawlins led Narraway into a small hospital ward where only one bed was occupied. A man lay slightly propped up on a pillow. His face was almost colourless and his cheeks were sunken, making the bones sharp and protruding. His skin was stretched, papery and fragile. He might have been any age from twenty to forty. The bedding was held up over a frame above his right leg, and where his left leg should have been.

Narraway wished immediately that he had not come, but it was too late to retreat. How did Rawlins deal with this sort of thing day after day, and stay sane?

Although they had moved with very little sound, Tierney must have sensed their presence because he opened his eyes and looked at Rawlins.

'Hello, Doc. Come to see if I'm still here?' He gave a very faint smile.

Rawlins smiled back at him. 'Only full-time patient I've got now. Have to see you,' he replied cheerfully. 'If I have nothing to do they might not pay me, then how will I buy a decent cigar?'

'That's what I'd really like,' Tierney said huskily. 'A decent cigar.'

'I'll bring you one,' Rawlins promised. 'But if you set the bed on fire then you can damn well lie on the floor.'

Tierney laughed. It was a rough, croaking sound. 'Like I'd know the difference! What've you got in this mattress? Sand?'

'Gunpowder,' Rawlins replied. 'So don't drop the ash either.' He gestured towards Narraway. 'This is a brand-new lieutenant, at least to Cawnpore. Tell him about the place. We have decent mangoes here. And tamarinds, if you like

61

them, or guavas. Nothing much else is worth anything.'

'Any news?' Tierney asked, still looking at Rawlins.

'Nothing that I've heard,' Rawlins replied. 'If we win, we'll tell you, I promise. If we lose, you'll find out anyway.' He gave a mock salute and left, walking back out again into the corridor, leaving Narraway alone by the bed.

Narraway lost his nerve to ask Tierney anything about the ambush of the patrol. It wouldn't make any difference to the trial anyway. It didn't matter where Dhuleep Singh had gone to or what he had told anyone. The murder of Chuttur Singh was enough to damn him.

'Where were you before here?' he asked conversationally.

'Delhi, God help me,' Tierney answered with a down-turned smile.

'I imagine it was pretty bad,' Narraway sympathised.

'All so bloody unnecessary,' Tierney replied, a trace of bitterness in his voice. 'The Indian soldier's a damn good man. If we'd just listened, instead of always thinking we knew everything better. Took their loyalty for granted. Damn idiots should have seen it coming. Stupid bloody mess! You?'

'Calcutta,' Narraway answered, thinking back to his arrival in India, confused, excited and afraid, hearing rumours of unrest already. 'Nearly a year ago. Thought I'd escaped the English winter!' He gave an ironic little laugh.

'Wouldn't mind a dusting of snow for

Christmas,' Tierney said. 'Where are you from? You sound like Home Counties, but that could be education, I suppose. I see you're a lieutenant, and you can't be more than twenty.'

For no particular reason, except something to say that had nothing whatever to do with India, mutiny, betrayal, wounds, blind stupidity, or trials, Narraway told him about his home in the softly rolling hills and wide valleys of Kent. He spoke of long rides on horseback over the Weald in the early morning, with the light on the grass, which rippled like water in the wind.

'So what are you doing out here in the dust, eating yet another curry and wasting time waiting for something to happen?' Tierney asked with a slight, stiff shrug of his shoulders, his eyes smiling.

'Escaping boiled cabbage, grey skies and biting wind with an edge of sleet in it,' Narraway replied cheerfully. 'And my father's wrath,' he added, with more truth to it than he wished.

'Which makes you much like the rest of us,' Tierney commiserated. 'Tell me more about Kent. Do you like the sea? I miss the sea, the smell of it, the cold, sharp spray on your face.'

Narraway stayed and talked for close to half an hour, until he could see that Tierney was exhausted. Even then he did not want Narraway to go. It was not until he unwittingly drifted off into a fitful sleep that Narraway walked softly away, grateful to have two feet to stand on, and no longer even aware of the smells of blood and carbolic and other odours he would rather not name.

He needed to be alone to think. He was too filled with emotion to have any plans worth the name.

The futility of it all overwhelmed him. Everyone knew at least something of the needless waste of the Crimean War, and questioned even the purpose of it. The army that had beaten Napoleon at Waterloo had rested too long on its laurels. It was now cumbersome and sorely in need of updating.

The idiocy of the grease on the bullets, which had become so hideously apparent at Dum Dum, and had fired a whole nation's mutiny, was still being excused by some. It was all avoidable! Was there no communication, no intelligence from which to foresee the errors and avoid them? Didn't the Army speak to the Government, or listen?

This was such a small part of the whole, and yet thinking of a few greased bullet cases, a rumour spread like wildfire, Narraway saw the enormity of even the smallest thoughtless act. One match could light the flames that consumed a nation, if the earth was already tinder dry, and no one had noticed that either.

For everyone's sake he must do the job that Latimer had commanded him. If he did not defend Tallis sufficiently well that the Court could say honestly that he had been properly represented, then his execution would in a sense also be murder. It would seem to others as if the regiment had convicted him in order to seem to have dealt with its own failure by vengeance rather than justice. They would look weak, not to be trusted; more than that, history would judge them to be without honour.

He continued walking, his feet making little sound on the earth and the thin, winter grass. He passed walls broken by shellfire. They were crumbling away now, over four months after the events. Ahead of him was a small, grassy mound with a few tangled bushes at the base of three trees. They were spindly, graceful. One was leafless and clearly dead. The other two still had rich evidence of life and in spring would no doubt have leaves, perhaps even blossom.

A few yards beyond was a round stone-rimmed well. There was nothing there with which to draw water, no covering to keep falling leaves out, no rope or pulley, no bucket of any kind.

He stopped and looked at it curiously. There was a desolation about it.

'You can't want to stand here, sir.'

He turned and saw Peterson a few feet away from him.

'Can't I?' He was curious. Peterson's face was white, his eyes hollow, without life. 'Are you ill?' he asked suddenly. 'You look . . . '

Peterson shivered. 'That's the well, sir — that well. You don't want to stand here.'

'That well?' Narraway repeated.

'Bibighar, where they massacred the women and cut them up, cut their heads off, and their . . . ' He made a helpless gesture, half indicating breasts. 'That's where they threw the bodies. Then their children after them. Scores of

65

them, not all of them even dead. Filled it right up. You don't want to stand here, sir.'

Narraway thought for a moment he was going to be sick. His stomach clenched and the outlines of the trees blurred in his vision. Sweat broke out on his skin. He turned to face Peterson.

'No,' he agreed. 'I didn't know it was . . . this well.' Carefully and a little unsteadily he put one foot in front of the other and walked away, Peterson a yard or so behind him.

He had heard the story in whispered pieces, conversations that trailed away into silence and pain. Cawnpore had been relieved on 17 July, about five months ago now, but the ghosts of the siege were everywhere. The heat had been appalling, over 120 degrees in the shade. The horrified soldiers of the relief had found the corpses of more than four hundred men, women and children.

In the Bibighar — the huge, two-roomed house in which Nana Sahib had kept the women of his pleasure during his occupation of the town — the soldiers had found the walls scarred low with the marks of sword cuts where women had been beheaded while on their knees. It was littered with hair and the combs that held it dressed, children's shoes, hats, bonnets, the torn pages of Bibles and prayer books. They had looked down to find their boots submerged in blood.

'I'd slit him open and pull his entrails out,' Peterson said quietly, staring into the distance. 'And burn them in front of him, still attached.'

Narraway found his voice with difficulty. 'Nobody would charge you with it,' he said, coughing a little to clear his throat. 'But if they did, I'd defend you for that. You wouldn't need any better skill than I have to get you off. I don't know how anybody here is still sane.'

'Maybe we aren't,' Peterson replied. 'I wonder sometimes if I am. I wake up in the middle of the night, and I can still smell it. Funny that, isn't it? I can't always see it, but I can smell it, and I can hear the flies. Do you believe in God?'

Narraway was about to answer automatically, then he stopped. Peterson deserved better than that. Narraway himself needed more than a trite response.

'Well, I certainly believe in hell,' he said slowly, selecting his words. 'So I suppose I must believe in heaven too. And if there's a heaven and a hell, then I think there must be a God. All this is unbearable if there isn't. But I suppose that's not a reason, is it?'

Peterson shook his head. 'It's not the same as good and evil. Nobody doubts that. But is there anybody in control of it? I wonder sometimes if it doesn't just happen, and that's all there is. Is there any sense, any justice? Or is it up to us to make it, and nobody else does the things we can't, or won't?'

'That's a hell of a question, Private Peterson. But I suppose the Bibighar well is as good a place as any to ask it.'

Narraway thought for a while. It was a place that demanded answers to such thoughts, not just for Peterson, or the Court that was set for

67

tomorrow, or for Tierney, or John Tallis. He needed it for himself.

Peterson waited.

'If there were anybody in control, you'd think they'd make a better job of it, I suppose,' Narraway began. 'What happened here seems beyond ordinary human evil. It's as if someone opened a door into something else. But if hell were not lower than anything a sane man can imagine, then maybe heaven wouldn't be higher than even our most exquisite dreams.'

Peterson shook his head slightly. 'Wouldn't you accept heaven a little lower if hell could be . . . not this bad?'

'I don't think anybody asked me,' Narraway replied seriously. 'But if they had, I don't know what I would have said. I didn't see the heaven part of it — only this.'

'But you believe in it?'

Narraway suddenly remembered the blue paper chain, and all the women who were going to celebrate Christmas, for their children. 'Yes, I do,' he answered. 'Lots of people do, no matter what happens. We pick up the pieces and start again, for the sake of those who believe in us. If we can do it, then the best in us is trusting in something, reaching towards something. We can't let them down.'

'God?' Peterson asked. 'Sir?'

'I think so. Something that is as good as this is awful. Believe it, at least until you wake up dead, and find it isn't true.'

Peterson's face relaxed in a smile. 'I didn't expect you to be so honest. Thanks. I'd still leave here, if I were you.'

Narraway agreed, and with a brief salute he walked away from the Bibighar and its ghosts.

★　★　★

Knowledge, that was the key. Narraway sat on the stone buttress of the old armoury, now little more than a pile of rubble. The wind was rising, cold-edged, tossing the leaves on the trees. Information was what mattered, and how it fitted together to form meaning, if only he could see it. Everything was a matter of putting the pieces into the right order.

One of the difficulties was that you never knew if you had all the pieces yet, or if something vital was still missing, something that formed the centre of the picture.

What had he overlooked that so far it all made no sense? He was a soldier, not a policeman, not a lawyer. But he should still be able to understand it if he tried hard enough. He knew the people, he knew the events. Did he know them in the wrong order? Was it something missing that was wrong, or one cornerstone point that was a lie? What one change would alter it all so it made sense?

There had been no one inside the prison except Chuttur and Dhuleep. The door opened only from the outside. Grant had found it closed, gone in and discovered the dying Chuttur, who told him Dhuleep had escaped — someone engineered his escape but he had not said who. Attwood and Peterson had then arrived, perhaps a minute later, and passed no one. They agreed with everything Grant said. Chuttur died without ever speaking again.

The three soldiers had gone looking for Dhuleep, but found only traces of his escape, signs of where he had been. The patrol had been ambushed and killed, all but Tierney.

The only man unaccounted for was Tallis. Tallis swore he was innocent. What was missing? What was the lie?

It had to be Tallis — didn't it?

What was the information, the knowledge that Narraway did not have? He hated the chaos that spread like madness across India, and the tiny piece of it that jumbled and boiled in his own mind, senselessly. He hated the internal darkness of it.

★   ★   ★

He was allowed in to see Tallis without question, although the guards' faces reflected a coldness, as if they imagined he were defending him because he wished to, not because he had been commanded. He hesitated, wanting to tell them how much it was against his will, then realised that would be childish. Half of what anybody did in the army was against their will. You still should do it to the best of your ability, and without complaining or trying to justify yourself. He was an officer; better than that was required of him. The fact that just over two years ago he had been a schoolboy was irrelevant. Many of these men had been soldiers, fighting, shot at, acting with courage and loyalty at eighteen. Respect had to be earned.

He thanked them and went into Tallis's cell.

Tallis stood to attention. It was only hours since Narraway had seen him, but he looked leaner, even greyer in the face. He was a man with only two or three days to live, and that shadow was stark in his eyes.

Time was too short for niceties, and at this point they would be a mockery. They stood because there was nothing in the cell to sit on, except the floor.

'At ease,' Narraway said, otherwise Tallis would be obliged to remain to attention. 'I've spoken to the three men who answered the alarm and found Chuttur Singh. He didn't name you, but he said there was a man who came in and took him by surprise, and let Dhuleep out, or words that amounted to that. And given the situation, that's the only answer that makes any sense. He couldn't have opened the door from the inside himself.'

'I know that,' Tallis said quickly. 'We all know there had to be someone else, but it wasn't me.' His voice was level but there was desperation in his eyes. 'I was counting bandages and what medicines we had left in the storeroom. I can't prove it because no one else knows what was there. I wouldn't have been counting them if I knew what was there myself! It's the only time I'm sorry we didn't have any poor devil in there sick!'

'Ever treated Dhuleep?' Narraway asked. 'Do you know anything about him? This is not time for medical confidences.'

'I suppose I could always invent something?' Tallis said with mock cheerfulness. 'How about rabies? I let him go so he could infect the entire mutineer army. No good? I could say . . . '

'Tallis!' Narraway snapped. 'I want to know if you know the damn man. Did you ever treat him?'

Tallis looked slightly surprised. 'Yes. He had a bunion on his left foot. I'm intimate with it. I could draw you a picture. Couldn't cure it, of course. Not a thing you can do for them. Cured his indigestion. It doesn't exactly rate as a friendship. I cure people I don't like exactly the same as people I do. It's what medicine is about.' He gave a sad, self-mocking smile. 'Just like you defend people whether you think they're guilty or not . . . '

Narraway was temporarily robbed of words. He had not intended to be so transparent. 'Give me anything to argue with!' he begged. 'What was Dhuleep like? Why did no one expect him to escape? Why was there only one guard? Who would want to help him? Who did he associate with? Who would want him free? If you didn't do it, then someone else did! For heaven's sake, man — help me!'

'Do you think I haven't lain awake trying to think?' Tallis asked. 'Nobody likes a telltale, but I'd outdo the best actor on stage with stories that'd curl your hair, if I knew any. I thought he might know something that was worth his freedom, but who would he sell it to? Latimer? Then I wondered if he was a double traitor, to us

72

and then to the mutineers. Maybe he was let go on purpose, like a disease, to spread lies. Anything to make sense of it.' He shrugged. 'But as far as I know, he was just one more Sikh soldier that seemed to be loyal. Some are, some aren't. We can't afford to do without the loyal ones. I mean, look at it!' He swung his arm around indicating the immeasurable land beyond the cell and the compound. 'We're a handful of white men, a few tens of thousands, half the world away from home, trying to govern a whole bloody continent. We don't speak their languages, we don't understand their religion, we can't stand their bloody climate and we have no immunity to their diseases. Yet here we are, and expecting to be liked! And we're all taken by surprise when they stick a knife into our backs. God help us, we're idiots!'

'Don't say that in court tomorrow,' Narraway said drily, although he was startled how much he agreed with him.

'Never let the truth spoil a good defence,' Tallis paraphrased with a crooked smile. 'I haven't got a good defence, except that I didn't do it. And I haven't an idea in hell who did. I'm trusting you because I haven't got anything else. If you'd asked me a month ago if I believed in some kind of divine justice, or even in a man-made honour, I'd have laughed at you, probably made a bad joke.' He shrugged his thin shoulders. 'If you don't believe in anything at all, you'd shoot yourself. Get it right, and at least that would be quick.'

Suddenly his face was totally serious. The

laughter vanished; even the self-mockery was gone. 'You see courage that's sublime, people enduring pain, disfigurement, losing parts of themselves so they'll never be whole again, and yet not complaining, still keeping the dignity that's inside them. It has nothing to do with being able to control your own body, or even your mind. People care for others, even when they know they're dying themselves. They keep faith even when it's idiotic, everything's gone, and you know it.'

Narraway wanted to shout at him to stop, but he couldn't. He had to listen, even to believe.

'I know they'll convict me, even though I didn't do it,' Tallis added, his eyes never leaving Narraway's. 'But I still believe you'll find a way to prove that. Unfair, isn't it?' He grinned. It was a brilliant, shining smile, as if in spite of all that his brain told him, he had a kind of happiness he refused to let go of. He would not accept reality. 'You should try being a doctor some time. See this after every battle, every skirmish. They carry them in one after another, people who look to you to save them, and you can't, but you try anyway. One thing you learn, Lieutenant: you can't tell who's going to live and who isn't. You learn there's something bigger than you, bigger than anything sense tells you. I believe in the impossible, good and bad. I've seen lots of it. I did not kill Chuttur Singh, or let Dhuleep go. I wasn't even there.'

Narraway wanted to have an answer, something brave and wise to say. He wished, with a hunger that consumed him, to believe in the impossible, and he could not. He did the only thing he could bear, he lied.

'Then I'll believe in miracles too,' he said quietly. 'I'll find one.'

He did not remain. He had already asked all the questions he could think of. No answer helped, they only reinforced the futility of it. He left the prison and walked outside into the dark. The vast night sky arched over him, brilliant with stars. The faint wind stirred through the branches of the few trees, a black lattice work against the sheen of light. And he felt just as boxed in, as locked and shackled as Tallis. There was no escape.

He walked for quite a distance. He knew that before he turned in he should report to Colonel Latimer, but he was putting it off as long as possible. He had learned nothing useful in the time he had been given to look into the case. Quite honestly, he did not believe any extension of the time would make a difference. It was putting off the inevitable, prolonging the misery for everyone, including Tallis himself.

He turned and went in the direction of the officers' mess where he knew Latimer would be at this time in the evening. Probably Busby and Strafford would be with him, which would make it worse.

He passed a couple of small buildings and heard someone tapping nails into wood. He wondered what they were making. Household furniture, mending a chair or a table? Or a toy for a child, a Christmas present? A wagon with wheels that turned, perhaps? He could dimly remember one in his own childhood. Only fifteen years ago he had been the right age to play with such a thing.

Would the widow's little boy have a wagon, or coloured bricks this Christmas? Perhaps Narraway could make sure that he did. He didn't have to give it to the boy himself; that might only embarrass her, make her feel obliged, and he did not want that. Would the boy even like a wagon? Wasn't it worth trying? The little girl, Helena, had given him the blue paper chain, certain that he would like it, because she did. He should find something for her too. He would have to ask somebody. A woman would know.

He stopped and knocked on the door of the building where the banging came from. After several moments a man with a leather apron on came to the door. 'Yes, sir?' he said politely. He was dark-skinned, black-haired, Indian.

'Are you a carpenter?' Narraway asked.

'No, I just mend things here and there. If you have a chair that is broken, perhaps I can help?'

'Actually . . . what I want is a small wooden wagon . . . for a child,' Narraway replied, feeling foolish.

The man looked surprised. 'You have a son? You want something for him for a gift, Sahib?'

'No . . . and yes. He's not my son, but he's lost his father. I just thought . . . ' He tailed off, his confidence draining away.

'I can do that,' the man said quietly. 'I will make you one. Come back in a few days. I have many small pieces of wood. And red paint. It will not cost much.'

'Thank you,' Narraway accepted. 'My name's Lieutenant Narraway. I'll be back. I'd like that very much.'

As he walked past the next open door he heard a woman inside, singing. Her voice was soft and filled with music. He had no idea who she was, but she was singing to someone she loved, of that he was certain. Probably it was a child. Reluctantly he moved on, out of earshot, towards the officers' mess.

At first Narraway was almost relieved not to see Latimer and had half-turned to go when he noticed Strafford, and then Latimer beside him. He pulled his tunic a little straighter and squared his shoulders, then walked across between the tables and chairs and rickety stools until he stood to attention in front of Latimer.

'Sir.'

Latimer turned towards him as if he had been expecting this moment, and not looking forward to it any more than Narraway himself.

'Are you ready, Lieutenant?' he asked. His face was pale and tired. He nursed a glass of whisky in his hand as if it could feel his touch, his fingers caressing it.

'Yes, sir,' Narraway replied. They both knew it was a lie, but it was the answer expected of him.

'You've spoken with Tallis?' Latimer pursued.

'Yes, sir.'

'Any help?'

'Not much.'

Latimer smiled; for a moment it softened the lines in his face. 'Like him?'

Narraway was not prepared for the question.

'Ah . . . yes, sir. I couldn't help it. Would have preferred not to.'

'If you'd said 'no', I wouldn't have believed you,' Latimer sighed. 'One thing you'll have to learn if you're going to make it in the army, Narraway, know when to lie to your superiors, and when not to. Sometimes we know the truth, but we don't want to hear it.'

'Sorry, sir. I didn't know this was one of them.'

'It isn't. Your judgement was quite right. He's a likeable man. We need the kind of humour he brings, and the unreason, the ability to hope when it makes no sense. I wish to hell it had been anybody else but him. You can't save him, but for God's sake, make it look as if you're trying.'

'Yes, sir.' Narraway felt stupid going on saying the same thing, but there was nothing else to add.

'Busby'll give you a hard time. Expect it, and don't lose your temper, no matter what he says. He lost a lifelong friend in that ambush. He'd served with Tierney a long time too. That's the fellow who lost a leg.'

'Yes, sir, I know. I spoke to him. A good man,' Narraway replied.

'Did you?' Latimer looked slightly surprised. 'Tell you anything useful?'

'No, sir. Just thought I should speak to him.'

'Well, you'd better go and get a decent night's sleep — or as decent as you can.'

'Yes, sir. Good night, sir.'

Latimer lifted a hand in a slight salute. 'Good night, Lieutenant Narraway!' Then: 'Did you

78

make any sense of it yet?' he asked suddenly.

Narraway felt the coldness deep inside him. 'No, sir, but I will.'

'That was the lie I wanted to hear,' Latimer said with a faint smile.

★ ★ ★

Narraway could not sleep. He lay on his cot. It was comfortable enough and better than many places in which he had slept perfectly well over the last year, including the ground, but restfulness eluded him. He turned one way then the other, sometimes with his eyes closed, sometimes staring up at the ceiling, which was pale from the starlight through the window. Tallis's face came back to his mind regardless of all his efforts to argue it away. It was an inescapable burden, suffocating him.

It was not only Narraway's career at stake, it was the whole regiment's honour, its belief in justice as an abstract, a perfect and beautiful thing that every man strove for. Except that that was nonsense. Some did, many merely used the word.

Narraway had not been among the soldiers who had relieved Cawnpore after the siege. He had been further north, but he had heard at least something of the horror of it. What the soldiers arriving had seen had driven them almost out of their senses. The vengeance had been appalling. No one had bothered with justice then. Murder had been called execution and the dead were everywhere. Could Tallis possibly not know that?

Had he not seen the emotion in the men, the stunned look in their eyes far deeper than mere tiredness, the wandering attention from time to time, even a certain clumsiness in movement as if they lacked coordination? The horror and the grief were too enormous to recover from in a few short months. Maybe they would never again be quite the same men as they had been before?

Right now, faced with an immediate decision of what to say in the trial in a matter of hours, Narraway dared not think about his own career in the future, but that time would come.

He could not win; it was only the measure of his loss that counted. Some would judge him for trying at all, even though the soldier in them would know he was obeying an order he could not refuse. Reason would defend him, but emotion would not.

Again and again he came back to reason. He could see very easily why Latimer needed to understand. It was not simply a matter of morale. Without understanding they would simply commit the same errors over and over again in the future. For all he knew, they might be committing them right now. He had to have knowledge!

What was he misreading? What pieces did he not see at all? Was there something in the puzzle that did not belong? He must have some plan before morning.

He went over it again in his mind, and came up with the same answer. There was no one it could have been, except Tallis. Tallis had sworn his innocence, and even Busby could come up with no reason at all why Tallis should have wanted Dhuleep to escape.

Reason — that was the missing piece.

He could not think of anything that would justify letting Dhuleep escape, or slashing Chuttur to death. The best that could be said was that it would also, in a way, satisfy himself. His hunger to see sense was growing more powerful, the need for an overall intelligence that promised future control of at least the most violent and chaotic of events.

He could hear no sound in the night except his own breathing, and the whine of an insect somewhere.

Then a thought struck him. Perhaps the act made no sense because it was not the result Tallis had intended? What if it were something quite different? Might he have known that Dhuleep had such information, and intended to kill him, and not Chuttur? The original charge against Dhuleep was not serious. In a few days he might well have been let go anyway.

How would Tallis have known that, and why not kill him in some more discreet way — medically? It would look like a natural death.

Or might Chuttur secretly have been a traitor as well? These days, nobody knew who was on which side. People crossed from one to another. Originally there were no sides at all. It was a mutiny, not a war with clearly defined lines.

Then why would Tallis not now say so? Did it involve someone else he could not betray? Were there further traitors he must not warn?

Narraway could not forget the man's trust. Would he spend the rest of his life measuring himself against this one failure? Would he even have the courage to fight his hardest for Tallis, knowing he could only lose? And when it was all over, would he have the courage to watch the hanging, knowing that he had been the one hope Tallis had had?

Why the hell did Tallis not trust him with the truth, and yet believe he would still help, bring off some kind of miracle? They did not even know each other. Narraway had never represented anyone at trial before; he had no reputation for such a thing.

Maybe it was not Narraway that Tallis trusted but British law? Then where the devil did he grow up that he did not know there were miscarriages of justice at home as well?

A trust in the British? After the atrocities on both sides of the mutiny, that would be absurd. And Tallis had surely seen the worst part of all that? He was a medical orderly — no one could show him or teach him horror that he had not already seen.

Narraway turned over again and pulled the blanket after him. He was cold and tired and his head was pounding, but he was no nearer sleep.

Maybe it was God Tallis believed in. That did not require reason. If circumstances were extreme enough, maybe it was all there was left. Tallis was a young man. He had chosen a noble path in life: the healing of others, even at times at the risk of his own life. If he had stayed in Britain he could have been comfortable, respected and safe. Maybe he had a right to expect something of God?

Was that the way he saw it? God would help him?

Why? God had not helped the thousands who had been murdered in the mutiny. He had not saved the women and children at the Bibighar well.

Did Tallis think he was special, to be saved when others were not? Why? Arrogance? Desperation? The impossibility of grasping and accepting the idea of one's own death?

He turned over again to the other side, then on to his back, eyes open, watching the starlight on the ceiling.

What did he believe in himself? What did he trust? That called for a harsh review. Shouldn't it be something he knew, without having to search for it?

He had been brought up to attend church. Everybody did. Did he believe in its teachings, its doctrine? Did he even believe in the God they taught?

He realised with a sudden chill, as if someone had snatched his blanket away, that he had never really looked far enough into himself to know. If he had to answer now, tonight, staring at the starlight on the ceiling of his bedroom in this battered and rather shabby house, did he believe in God?

He certainly did not disbelieve. But not in the grand and rather distant God of the churches he had been to. If He was a God for everyone, then

He must be equally so for the Indian, or the Chinaman or the black man of Africa. Anything else was an affront not only to the intelligence but even more so to the morality.

And yes, that God he did believe in. Maybe it was because he needed to. For everything to be pointless, accidental and without love or purpose, was a sterility he would not entertain. It made no room for laughter, beauty, or even love. It did not allow for hope, for that in man that forgives. Nor, perhaps, for that in woman that nurtures endlessly, and will sacrifice herself to save her children, without ever thinking of the cost.

For what did he trust God, the good parent?

Mercy? Perhaps at Judgement Day, if such existed, but there was scant evidence of it now.

Justice? There was scant evidence of that either. But then if there were, if good were rewarded with good, and evil with evil, would either of them really exist? Would there be anything more than enlightened self-interest? Not virtue, simply barter.

That was a world so ugly, so barren and eventually hideous that he thrust away the idea. It was a kind of universal death.

No justice then; except what man himself strove to make.

No biblical promise that he could recall had ever said that it would be without pain, loss, injustice: simply that in the end it would be worth it.

Faith? Certainly, but blind faith that did not expect immediate reward, a trust that did not

84

look to be vindicated and explained to at every step along the way.

Was that what he believed? Yes, perhaps it was.

Could he live up to it? That remained to be seen.

But a plan was beginning to form in his mind, a way to discover the missing pieces that would make sense of both Tallis's act, and his silence now. It must lie in the characters of Dhuleep and Chuttur themselves, something Tallis knew of them and Latimer did not.

Gradually he drifted to an uneasy sleep, filled with fading and ballooning nightmares, sometimes acutely sharp.

* * *

The trial of John Tallis began that following morning. No one attended except those who were necessary for the process to be legal. Latimer had wanted as little attention brought to the details as possible. He sat at the top table with two other officers Narraway did not know. Busby was at a small table on one side, with his papers spread in front of him, Narraway on the other.

Tallis, in uniform rather than his medical working clothes, sat beside Narraway. They had no suitable handcuffs or chains in which to keep him, but there were armed soldiers at the door, and in the room beyond where various witnesses were waiting. A couple of junior officers appeared to be in charge of events as ushers, and a third sat at a small table off to one side, pen poised to record what was said. How on earth he would keep up with it Narraway had no idea.

As soon as the formalities were dealt with, Busby began by calling his first witness. It was clear even from the brisk way in which he spoke, from the neatness of his uniform and the immaculate way his hair was brushed, that he intended to observe the letter of the law.

Of course he knew he was going to win. There was no battle, only the pretence of one.

Grant was called. He came in straight-backed but looking curiously tired as if he had difficulty keeping his attention on the matter in hand. He faced Busby, waiting.

Busby stood, speaking quietly, as if there were only the two of them in the room.

'I'm sorry to have to take you through all this again, Corporal Grant,' he said gently. 'I'm sure you understand the necessity. We must do justice here, not only to the dead, and their families, but to the living. It must also be seen by others, far beyond this regiment, or Cawnpore itself, that murder will be punished, fairly and justly, and that our actions are not taken out of revenge.'

'Yes, sir,' Grant responded, straightening his shoulders a little more.

Step by step, Busby led him through hearing the alarm, dropping what he was doing and running towards the prison. He had him describe exactly what he did, what he saw, not dwelling on unnecessary horror to give Narraway a chance to object that he was playing on emotions rather than facts. Everyone in the room had seen enough violence not to need pictures painted for them in words. And perhaps they were already overloaded with pity and grief. There is only so much even a soldier hardened in war can bear before it ceases to make impact on the mind.

'Thank you,' Busby said when Grant had come to the end of his description. 'Please wait there in case Lieutenant Narraway has anything to ask you.'

Narraway stood up slowly. He was disgusted with himself to find that he was shaking. It was absurd. He was going to lose. The battle was over before it began. The best he could hope for was a reason that made sense of it.

He cleared his throat. 'Corporal Grant, when I spoke to you yesterday, asking you about this tragedy, you told me that Chuttur Singh was fatally wounded when you found him.'

'Yes, sir,' Grant said too quickly. He also was nervous, his body tight under the fabric of his uniform, his shoulders high and rigid. He had liked both Chuttur Singh and Tallis. This was clearly painful for him.

'We appreciate that there was nothing you could do for him, Corporal,' Narraway said as gently as he could. 'You said to Captain Busby that Chuttur Singh told you the prisoner had escaped and that recapturing him was more important than anything else, is that correct?'

Busby moved impatiently.

Latimer held up his hand to silence him.

'Yes, sir,' Grant agreed.

'He told you to leave him and pursue the prisoner, Dhuleep Singh?' Narraway persisted.

'Because he knew the route and times of the patrol?'

'Yes, sir.'

'Do you know how he knew that?'

Grant looked slightly surprised. 'No, sir.'

'Yet you did not question it?'

'No, sir.'

'You told me that Chuttur had said someone had come into the prison from outside and attacked him. I asked you if Chuttur Singh had told you who the other man was, and you told me he had not. Is that correct?'

Grant let his breath go slowly. 'Yes, sir. That is correct. I . . . I don't think he knew.'

'It isn't that he told you, and for some reason or other you are concealing it?' Narraway pressed.

Busby rose to his feet. 'Colonel Latimer, this is — '

Latimer held up his hand. 'Perfectly fair, Captain. Thank you, Lieutenant Narraway. We have established that Chuttur Singh did not tell Corporal Grant who attacked him, and we may safely presume it was because he did not know. Have you anything further, Lieutenant, perhaps regarding Dhuleep Singh's knowledge of the patrol?'

'Not at this time, thank you, sir.' Narraway sat down with relief washing over him, his knees feeling like water.

Busby then called Attwood, who said much the same as Grant had. However, his words were not so identical as to make it seem as if they had conferred. Narraway could think of nothing to contest, and did not want to risk making it any worse. Attwood's distress was clear, as was his anger and contempt.

Finally Busby called Peterson, who added nothing of value, except in his careful and clearly honest description of how he had left the prison block and gone searching for Dhuleep Singh. It was he who had found faint traces of blood showing the path of escape. Busby obtained all the details from him, making the scene seem real and urgent, terribly familiar to those listening. It was Peterson who had gone in the direction of the Bibighar Gardens, and the well.

'Did you search the Bibighar building for this man?' Busby asked.

Peterson was white-faced. 'Yes, sir. He wasn't there.' He was shaking very slightly.

'You looked inside the house?' Busby persisted. 'You didn't avoid it . . . because . . . '

Narraway knew what Busby was doing and he could not bear it. He stood up, facing Colonel Latimer.

'Sir, Captain Busby is suggesting that Private Peterson failed in his duty because of the horror of what happened there, and possibly his own personal grief. Private Peterson has told the Court that he looked. He is an honourable man and a good soldier. He is not charged with anything and should not have his courage or his honesty brought into question here.'

There was a murmur of approval from the man to Latimer's right, and both the men acting as ushers nodded.

'Thank you,' Latimer nodded at Narraway.

'Captain Busby, we are satisfied that Private Peterson has answered your question. No one found Dhuleep Singh, as is only too evident to all of us. If you have nothing further to ask him, then when Lieutenant Narraway has spoken, we will adjourn for luncheon.'

Busby sat down, his face faintly flushed.

'Thank you, sir,' Narraway acknowledged. 'I think what happened after the alarm was sounded is very clear. I have nothing useful to ask Private Peterson.'

Latimer nodded, his face expressionless.

'We are adjourned until two o'clock,' he told them.

Narraway left alone, not that he was offered much choice. As he walked away across the open space, the cold wind striking him even through his uniform, he felt something of a panic. No one openly snubbed him, but neither did anyone speak to him. In a way he was grateful. He needed time alone in which to think. The answer did not lie with any of the soldiers questioned this morning. He was becoming more and more convinced that it had to do with Dhuleep and Chuttur, and the information about the patrol. If only he could grasp the missing fact that would make sense of it. How did Dhuleep know? Was Chuttur involved after all? Was it Chuttur who knew, and was tortured for it?

That answer did not help Tallis at all. He was still missing the key!

In the officers' mess he found a place in a far corner and sat eating absent-mindedly. He had no hunger, but he knew that if he took nothing

90

he would regret it later. How could something as rich as a curry seem tasteless?

He left the plate half-finished and went to look for the sergeant who had spent most time with the Sikh troop, Gholab Singh. He found him in a small office in one of the barracks still left largely intact.

'Yes, sir?' Gholab Singh said courteously, rising to his feet.

Narraway introduced himself and told the sergeant to be at ease.

'What can you tell me about Dhuleep Singh?' he asked as soon as the man was seated again. 'Other than what I have read in his army record.'

Gholab looked uncomfortable. 'I am ashamed for him, sir,' he said quietly. 'To rebel openly I cannot fault him for, at least not greatly. But to betray behind the back is another thing altogether different. He is a sneaky bastard, sir. Very clever. Always listening and adding up in his mind, that one.'

'It doesn't surprise you that he knew the times and routes of the patrol?' Narraway asked.

Gholab shook his head sadly. 'He is a tricky one. He darkens all our names.'

'And Chuttur Singh?' Narraway asked.

'A good man,' Gholab said without hesitation. 'I know his brother, and his cousin. Good men, all of them. Maybe a bit too trusting. Not a bad fault in a man. Better than deceit.' He shook his head. 'Cousin to a snake, Dhuleep. May he eat the dust.'

Narraway stayed a little longer, asking questions as they came to his mind, but Gholab could tell him nothing further of use. He had no idea if either Chuttur or Dhuleep had any personal acquaintance with Tallis.

★ ★ ★

The afternoon began with Busby calling Dr Rawlins. The room sat in total silence. Tallis stared white-faced into the distance as Rawlins described the injuries to Chuttur Singh.

Busby's expression was one of shock and deep grief. No one could imagine it assumed. Each man in the room had seen the injuries of war, seen soldiers cut down beside them, friends, people with whom they had shared jokes and food, and dreams of home. This was different. Civilised men fought for their ideals, for their countries, sometimes whether they believed them right or wrong. Even barbarians were loyal to their own. To betray and slash to death a man who had trusted you was murder, and as such deserved no mercy. Indeed, if the law were to stand for anything, if it were even to survive, such an act must be punished. And Tallis knew that.

'Did Chuttur Singh fight back, Dr Rawlins?' Busby asked.

'There were deep slashes on his arms, which suggest he may have tried to defend himself,' Rawlins replied. 'And I believe there was a degree of blood on his own sword. I can't tell you what that means because his sword may have been used against him.'

'To sum up,' Busby said grimly. 'There was a

92

blow to the back of his head, hard enough to have stunned him momentarily, after which he was hacked to death with at least fifteen violent blows from a sword.'

'Yes,' Rawlins said with a catch in his voice.

'He bled to death?' Busby pressed.

'Yes.'

'Have you ever seen wounds like this before?' Busby continued.

Rawlins looked, if anything, even paler. 'Of course I have,' his voice grated. 'I was with the regiment that relieved Cawnpore after the siege. I stood almost ankle-deep in blood in the Bibighar where the women and children were hacked to pieces. Some of them were the families of my friends. I refuse to describe it for you. Those who saw it will never forget, and those who did not can look at the faces of those who did, and thank God for their escape.'

Busby looked at him with surprise, then glanced around at the other men in the room. Narraway followed his eyes and saw what he must also have seen. Every other man there had, at one time or another, received help from Rawlins. He had relieved their pain, watched with them through times of agony that could not be helped, comforted them when they feared maiming or death, mourned with them over loss. Busby would be a fool to challenge him.

'And the men of the patrol that was ambushed,' he said, changing his line of approach. 'Did you see their bodies when they were brought home . . . those that were?'

'They were buried where they fell,' Rawlins

replied. 'The two who were alive they brought with them, the best they could. Yes, I saw them. One died on the way back. The other looks as if he will recover, but he has lost the greater part of his leg.'

'They too were hacked to pieces,' Busby said, making it a conclusion rather than a question.

'They were ambushed and died in battle,' Rawlins snapped. 'You have no business, sir, to suggest that they did not fight back.'

Busby retreated. 'I apologise. I did not mean to imply such a thing at all. They were surprised, betrayed, but I imagine they took a good few of the enemy with them, unlike poor Chuttur Singh, who was betrayed in quite a different manner, and outnumbered two to one.'

Rawlins said nothing.

Busby moved only slightly. The room was small and there was no space to spare. Nevertheless, he already appeared to feel cramped.

'Is there anything else that you can tell us of this terrible event that might help us bring the matter to resolution and allow justice to be done, and the rest of us to be certain that we have reached the truth and wronged no one?'

Rawlins leaned forward a little, staring at Busby.

'Captain, it is not my job to judge any man, only to heal him if I can. I do not know what happened in that prison, who did it or why. I have told you what the injuries were to Chuttur Singh, after he was brought to the medical wing.

I cannot deduce anything more than I have already told you.'

'Thank you, Dr Rawlins. I had assumed as much.' Busby seemed about to add something further, then changed his mind and turned to Narraway. His expression was bland, polite. One might almost have thought he pitied him, except for a bright spark of anger in his eyes.

Narraway rose to his feet knowing that this was his last chance. He still had a small, gnawing pain inside him that he could not ignore. What if Tallis were innocent? What if there were still some different question none of them had even thought of, because the answer was one they could not bear?

He turned to Rawlins. He was limited now. This was not his witness — he could only revisit the issues Busby had raised.

'How long have you been a surgeon with the regiment, sir?'

Busby was still standing. 'Are you questioning Dr Rawlins' qualifications?' he said incredulously.

'Of course I'm not!' Narraway said extremely tartly. 'I am trying to establish his very considerable expertise. Do you think I should be questioning his qualifications?' He invested the same haughty disbelief into his own voice.

'For God's sake, man!' Busby exploded.

Latimer banged on the desk. 'Captain Busby! We will not have the Lord's name taken in vain in this court. We may be far from home, and in considerable danger, but that is all the greater reason to conduct ourselves with dignity. Will you please allow Lieutenant Narraway to ask his questions. If they are inappropriate then I shall tell him so.'

A flash of anger spread up Busby's face but he sat down.

Narraway was about to thank Latimer, then thought better of it. It would be rubbing in the point, probably unwisely. He merely inclined his head and turned again towards Rawlins.

'How long have you been a surgeon with this regiment, sir?' he repeated.

'Seven and a half years,' Rawlins replied.

'And have you always had medical orderlies, such as John Tallis?'

'Yes, of course.'

'How long have you had John Tallis, specifically?'

'Approximately two years.'

'How has his conduct been, during that time?' Narraway could feel his heart pounding in his chest and his breath catching. He did not know what Rawlins' answer would be.

Rawlins stood a little straighter, squaring his shoulders. A tiny muscle ticked in his temple. His fair skin was sunburned, in places badly. He looked desperately tired.

'I found him undisciplined,' he said quietly. 'His sense of humour was unreliable, to put it at its kindest. He was frequently insubordinate. He was also the best medical orderly I have ever had, and I tried to encourage him to qualify as a doctor. He is highly skilled. He never gave up on saving a man's life, or attempting to save a limb. His compassion is extraordinary. He drove some of the more rigid officers to distraction, but I never met an ordinary man, Indian or white, who did not like him. I realise that that is not necessarily what you want to hear, but it is the truth.'

At the table, Latimer closed his eyes. His face was bleak, reflecting the hurt of betrayal that he felt, and that he knew was felt even more deeply in Rawlins.

Narraway did not know what to say. The air in the room seemed too heavy to breathe. His own mouth was dry. He could not look at Tallis. Rawlins had clearly not only thought unusually highly of Tallis, he had liked the man. His betrayal was personal perhaps even more profoundly than it was professional, or to the army and the country they both served.

Everyone was looking at Narraway, waiting for him to continue.

He gulped. He must say something.

'Did Corporal Tallis know Dhuleep Singh, as far as you are aware? Did he ever mention him, or did you see them together, Dr Rawlins?'

'No.'

'Can you imagine any reason whatever why Tallis should rescue Dhuleep Singh?'

'No.'

'Corporal Tallis is charged with this crime not because we believe he did such a thing, simply that we cannot believe that anyone else did. It is an accident of exclusion and not something we understand or can trace back to any behaviour of Corporal Tallis. Do you know of any other reason why we should think him guilty?'

'No.'

'Had he any hatred towards any of the men on the patrol that was ambushed?'

Rawlins was startled. 'Good God, no!'

'Did he even know who they were? Is he given that information?'

'No! We deal with them when they come back, not before they go,' Rawlins said bitterly. 'I don't know what the hell you're trying to suggest, but it's rubbish.'

'That is exactly what I am trying to suggest,' Narraway answered. 'There is some major element to this that we have not yet grasped.'

'If you are looking for sense in war, then you are even younger and more naive than I thought,' Rawlins said wearily. 'If you outlive the disease, it will cure itself.'

Narraway could think of nothing to say to that. He thanked Rawlins and sat down.

It was still early but Busby asked permission to delay calling Major Strafford until the following day, because he had a great deal of evidence to give. There might be a way, with some consideration, of shortening it without impairing the course of justice. Latimer agreed, and adjourned by half-past four.

Narraway walked out into the waning afternoon. He felt dazed, as if he had been in a physical fight that he was fortunate to escape from with no more than bruises and aching limbs. He had only this evening in which to come up with any witness to call for a defence when Strafford was finished testifying as to his investigation, which found that only Tallis could have been guilty.

Tallis himself was no help. He still insisted that he had no idea who could have killed Chuttur Singh, only that it had not been he.

Unless he could find that missing piece tonight, Narraway had nothing left except to challenge the witnesses Strafford's questioning produced. He could imagine how successful that was likely to be. No one was going to admit mistakes or go back on what they had first said. Continual repeating of it would have made it indelible in their minds, even if it had originally been tentative. Uncertainty would be wiped out by saying over and over again 'I saw', or 'I was there'. Even if doubt came, who would admit it now, with the Court looking on, and the whole regiment watching?

He was walking across the open space beyond the rooms where the trial was held. The sky in the east was darkening and little whispers of wind were stirring up eddies in the dust. Children were shouting in the distance, playing a game of some sort. A group of women stood close together, heads bent as they talked. Someone laughed: a soft, startlingly agreeable sound with no cruelty in it, only amusement.

'Narraway!' a voice called out abruptly from behind him.

He turned and saw Strafford a dozen yards away, moving quickly, his boots sending up spurts of dust.

'Yes, sir?' Narraway answered obediently. This was a confrontation he would dearly like to avoid, but Strafford outranked him and he had no escape.

Strafford reached him and stopped. He looked awkward, but the muscles were tight in his jaw and clearly he was not going to be put off.

'I intend to call the witnesses tomorrow who can rule out every man in Cawnpore, apart from Tallis,' he said without preamble. 'Don't drag this out any longer than you have to, for decency's sake. You can question each one as much as you like, and I appreciate you have to make it look as if you are making some attempt to defend the man. The law requires it. But you're new here — relatively new to India, for that matter. These men have been through hell. Every one of them has lost people he served with, people who've stood side by side with him in the face of the enemy.' He swallowed. 'Maybe you don't know what that means yet . . . '

Narraway stiffened. 'I'm not a lawyer, sir, I'm a soldier,' he said sharply. 'I've fought in the line just like anyone else. I've seen men die, and worse than that, I've seen them horribly wounded. I don't mean to be insubordinate, sir, but you have no grounds and no right to assume that all I do is defend soldiers in a back room in some military post. I'm doing this because I was ordered to, not because I chose it.'

'I know you did, Narraway, damn it!' Strafford said angrily. 'Who the hell do you think chose you? Latimer doesn't know you from the clerk who writes up the dispatches home.'

'Then he should bloody well look at the pips on my shoulders!' Narraway snapped.

100

Strafford almost smiled, then cut it off. 'Then would you prefer it if I said he doesn't know you from any other newly commissioned young officer fresh off the boat? I do, at least by repute.'

Narraway's heart sank. Strafford's brother again, the whole school record, the teasing, some of it less than good-natured, the inner contempt from the 'swot' who preferred classics to sports — except cricket. Narraway had been considerably better at cricket than Strafford Minor.

'Is that why you suggested to Colonel Latimer that he have me defend Tallis?' Narraway asked bitterly.

Strafford's eyebrows rose. 'Did you think I picked your name out of a hat? Of course it is. You're a stubborn bastard and you won't be beaten until you can see it so close in front of you you'll hit your nose if you take another step. Every man, no matter what he's accused of, deserves someone to speak for him. But right here and now, in this gutted town with its blood still reeking in the ground, we need to be sure we're hanging the right man, and then we need to do it quickly. Fight, by all means, but when you're beaten, which will be tomorrow, give up. Apart from anything else, don't give Tallis false hope. That's like a cat playing with a mouse. Let the end be quick and clean.'

Narraway looked at him, searching his face. He saw dislike in it, but not deceit.

'Are you absolutely certain Tallis is guilty?' he asked.

'Yes, I am,' Strafford replied without hesitation. 'I've looked into every other possibility, and

101

it could have been no one else. Damn it, Narraway, the man may be an insubordinate clown, but he's one of the best medical orderlies I've ever seen. Men respect him. He's probably saved as many lives over the last couple of years as Rawlins himself. Do you think I'd pin this on him if there were any other man it could have been? I want the truth — and I wish this weren't it — but it is.'

'Why?' Narraway said stubbornly. 'Why would Tallis rescue Dhuleep Singh? They didn't even know each other. If they did, you'd have produced a witness to say so.'

'I don't know,' Strafford admitted, miserable, but not disconcerted. 'Why do people do half the desperate or idiotic things they do? When you've been here another year or two you won't ask questions like that. Where were you during the summer? Not here! Not watching men you know dying of heatstroke or cholera, getting weaker day by day, sharing what food and water there was, protecting the women, desperate to save them. You weren't here crouching behind that pathetic wall of earth with nothing to shield you but a few bits of wood planking and some boxes, knowing that devil Nana Sahib was massing his hordes around you, growing closer every hour.'

Narraway wanted to interrupt him, but he dared not.

'Some of these men have seen hell in a way few people ever do, even in nightmare or with the horrors of madness,' Strafford went on. 'Look in their faces sometime, Lieutenant. Look in their eyes, then come back and ask me why they do crazy things, or forget who they are or why they're here. Imagine what Tallis has seen, and ask me if he could have gone mad and done something that makes no sense. Maybe he thought Chuttur Singh was Nana Sahib, or some other monster who cut up women and children. Maybe he simply went mad. I don't know. I just know that no one else could have done it. Believe me, I wish they could have. I tried to find any other answer.'

Narraway felt as if he had suddenly tripped and fallen, or the ground had risen up and struck him. Of course men who had endured what these men had could not be expected to keep the grip on sanity that men could sitting comfortably at home in a world that obeyed the laws of civilisation.

Tallis's clear blue eyes did not look insane. Desperate, perhaps, lit with an occasional, wild, mocking humour, but was that madness or the ultimate sanity? The only way to survive might be to take a minute at a time, laugh when you could, weep when you had to.

'I saw the bodies of the men on the patrol,' Strafford went on, his voice cracking from his effort to control it. 'They were cut to bits too. I knew every one of them. I'm the one who had to tell their wives, lie a little and say it was quick, pretend they hadn't bled to death out there, knowing no one would come for them, perhaps no one even find them, before the animals had destroyed everything that was human.'

'I spoke to Tierney,' Narraway said. 'Actually I

spoke to him for quite a long time. Told him about Kent where I come from, and he told me about his home. But you're right, sir, I'm not going to give up until I don't have another step to go.'

Strafford's face was grim. 'My brother said you were a stubborn sod.'

'Yes, sir,' Narraway replied, standing to attention. 'I don't suppose you want my opinion of him?'

'No, I bloody don't!' Strafford's face eased a fraction. 'I've got my own, better informed than yours.'

Narraway relaxed a fraction, but not quite enough for Strafford to be certain of it, he hoped.

Strafford stared at him for a moment, then turned and walked away. He disappeared in another swirl of dust as the wind eddied more sharply, the bare branches of the trees above him clattered and dry seed pods fell onto the ground.

Narraway also turned, but he walked instead further away from the shattered barracks and the intrenchment, the Bibighar Gardens and the clustered outbuildings and the beginning of the houses. He must think of something to say tomorrow. Strafford Minor had said he was stubborn, but not fit to make a good soldier, all brains and no courage, no steel in the soul. He knew that because he had said it to his face, at Eton.

Well, Narraway would prove to his brother that Strafford Minor was wrong.

In the morning Busby called Major Strafford to give evidence. He began by establishing that it was Strafford who had been commanded to investigate the murder of Chuttur Singh, which had allowed Dhuleep Singh to escape.

Busby stood in the centre of the small space between the table where Latimer sat with the other officers on either side of him, the place where the witness sat, and the tables behind which were Busby himself on one side, and Narraway on the other.

Busby drew in a deep breath. 'I regret the necessity for going into detail in this, but you were the officer entrusted with conducting this investigation into an act that has cost the lives of ten men, and will yet take the life of whoever is guilty of perpetrating it. Colonel Latimer has known you and your record for years, but his companion judges may be less familiar with exactly what manner of man you are. I say this because we are going to accept your honour, integrity and diligence as evidence of other men's actions, and pass our verdict accordingly.'

Strafford did not reply.

'It is a matter of record that you have served in the Indian Army for eleven years, with distinction. Were you here during the siege last summer?'

Strafford stiffened and his face paled.

'Yes.'

'You must have seen an appalling amount of suffering and death.'

'Yes.'

'During that time did you know the surgeon, Dr Rawlins?'

'Of course.'

'And Corporal Tallis, his medical orderly?'

Strafford was clearly distressed by the question. He licked his lips and coughed before replying.

'Of course I did. Before you ask me, he was an excellent orderly, often performing duties far beyond the requirements of his office or his training. Any man who was there will tell you that.' He took a deep breath. 'Believe me, I hate having to conclude that he was guilty of attacking Chuttur Singh and allowing Dhuleep to escape. I did everything I could to find any other solution at all. I failed, because there is no other.'

Busby stood ramrod stiff, carefully avoiding Narraway's eyes, or Latimer's.

'Major Strafford, I need to ask you, so no one is in any doubt whatsoever regarding your personal feelings. Have you at any time had cause to dislike Corporal Tallis? We are all aware that on occasion he has been known to be . . . insubordinate, to have a sense of humour that is somewhat unfortunate, given to rather childish practical jokes on those he considers to be . . . stiffer in their command than he judged to be warranted. Has he ever played any of these rather childish jokes on you? Perhaps caused others to have less respect for you than is right? In other words, have you ever been the butt of his humour? Have you been laughed at, made fun of, your authority belittled?'

A dull flush spread up Strafford's lean face.

'For God's sake, man!' he all but choked on his words. 'We were both there at the end of the siege when Mrs Greenway came with the note from Nana Sahib offering on oath and treaty to give safe passage for the wounded, the women and the children, across the Ganges and then to Allahabad. In return he asked and was given all the money, stores and guns in the intrenchment.' His voice shook and he had difficulty continuing.

Narraway sat frozen, not in misery for Tallis, but for Strafford himself.

Busby waited.

Strafford controlled himself with a fierce effort, drawing in breath again and again. His face was ashen.

'On the morning of the 27th those of us left went from the intrenchment to the boats. There were Indian soldiers lining the banks.'

Busby shifted his weight. No one else in the room made even the slightest sound.

'You know what happened after that,' Strafford said, his voice so constricted in his throat that he could barely form the words. 'Tanta Topee ordered the bugle sounded, then two guns were pulled out of concealment and opened fire on the boats, with grapeshot, followed by the muskets.' The tears were running freely down his face now and he made no effort to conceal them. 'The thatch on the boats caught fire. The wounded and the helpless were burned to death. Some of the women, including my own wife, leaped into the river, with their children. They too were shot, or cut down by the sabres of the troopers who rode their horses into the water and slaughtered all but a few. The men who made it to the shore were killed there, the women and children taken prisoners.'

Latimer spoke at last. 'Nothing we can say will ease such horror. It is all a man needs to know of hell. I presume you have some purpose, Captain Busby, in obliging Major Strafford to relive his loss?'

Busby swallowed. 'Yes, sir. Major Strafford, during all this horror, and afterwards, what was Corporal Tallis's part, to your knowledge?'

Narraway was stunned. He had no idea what to do for the best. The course of the trial had slipped uncontrollably out of his hands. He looked at Tallis, and saw the tears on his face also, unashamed. He barely even blinked.

'He was with the wounded and among the last to embark,' Strafford answered. 'He did everything he could to help those further attacked. No man exhibited more selfless courage than he did.'

'So it must hurt and dismay you, as much as it does Dr Rawlins, to be forced to come to the conclusion that he, and only he, could have murdered Chuttur Singh?'

'Yes.'

Busby gave a slight shrug. 'Just in case anybody should think of it, is there any chance that Chuttur Singh was part of that hideous betrayal? Could Tallis have had revenge for that massacre in his mind?'

'No,' Strafford said flatly. 'Chuttur Singh was

108

loyal all his life. I know that for a fact. No one could have thought differently.'

'Thank you. Now let us continue with your detailed evidence of the day of Chuttur's murder and Dhuleep's escape,' Busby resumed. 'What evidence did you find that immediately implicated anyone?'

'None,' Strafford replied. 'Chuttur Singh had died without naming anyone, and the men who answered the alarm were too late to catch sight of anyone, even when they went after Dhuleep.'

'So what did you do?' Busby asked. They all knew what Strafford was going to say. This was only the means of opening the way for him.

Strafford sounded tired, and there were lines of fatigue in his face. 'I started questioning all the other men who had been on duty, or off-duty but in the general area at the time. They could all account for their whereabouts, except Corporal Tallis.' His jaw was tight as if every muscle were clenched.

Busby looked apologetic. 'Since Corporal Tallis has denied any involvement in either the murder or the escape, I'm afraid that obliges me to ask you for the details of your investigation. Lieutenant Narraway has informed me that he will not accept your assurance, as I had hoped he might, and save us this miserable exercise. God knows, we have enough else to do.'

Narraway rose to his feet, driven by anger rather than sense. 'Is Captain Busby suggesting that we hang a man for a crime of which he may be innocent, in order to save the time it takes to go through the procedure of a trial, sir?'

Latimer's lips thinned and his hands on the table top were rigid. 'Of course not!' he snapped, then turned to Busby. 'Captain, your choice of words was clumsy, to put it at its kindest. It is you who are wasting time with grandstanding. Move on.'

Busby flushed with anger. He dared not retaliate, but neither would he apologise. He turned to Strafford again.

'Would you please give us an account of the various steps you took in your investigation, and how you ruled out all the other possibilities, apart from Corporal Tallis.'

In a flat voice Strafford obeyed, listing all the men he had confirmed were in the immediate area of the prison. He had a sheet of paper with names and he read them aloud.

'We know to the minute the time of the escape,' he continued. 'Most of these men were within sight of several people, and it was a simple matter to be certain beyond any doubt at all that they could not have been anywhere near the prison. In all cases the officer in charge at the time will swear to those accounted for, if you wish?'

Before Busby could say anything, Latimer spoke.

'If that satisfied you, Major Strafford, it satisfies the Court. Who did it leave unaccounted for?'

Strafford looked at his list. 'Corporal Reilly, Lance-Corporal McLeod, Privates Scott, Carpenter and Avery, and Corporal Tallis, sir.'

'Thank you. So that Lieutenant Narraway

might question them also, if he feels there is some point, perhaps we had better hear from them directly.' He glanced sideways at Narraway, as if to be certain the Court knew that it was Narraway who was dragging out the proceedings unnecessarily.

'Yes, sir, if you please,' Narraway replied as if it were Latimer who had asked.

Scott was the first called. In response to Busby's careful direction he accounted for his duties and his movements on the day of Chuttur's death. He had been across the open yard and around a dogleg from the prison. But anyone coming or going would have had to pass him, because that was the only access to the front, and there was no door at the back of the makeshift prison.

'What were you doing, Private Scott?'

'Working on mending a storeroom, sir. Door and windows had been smashed by shellfire during the siege. I was making it weatherproof again.'

'With your back to the courtyard, then?' Busby asked.

'No, sir. During that time I was making a new frame for the door. Had the wood up on a bench of sorts, planing it to fit.'

'So you could see anyone passing in either direction?'

'Yes, sir.'

'Could anyone see you?'

'Yes, sir. Lance-Corporal McLeod and Private Avery.'

'And no one passed you? You swear to it?'

111

'Yes, sir.'

'And you were there for that entire hour, Private Scott?'

'Yes, sir. It took me longer'n that to finish.'

'And could you see Corporal Reilly from where you were?'

'Yes, sir.'

'Did he move at all?'

'Yes, sir. 'E came over ter me ter see 'ow I were doing, an' 'e told me as I weren't doin' it right. 'E showed me 'ow to.'

'And then what?' Busby pressed.

''E went off be'ind me, to see 'ow the rest were gettin' on. Then 'e came back.'

'In the direction of the prison block?'

'No, sir, other way, back towards the river.'

'Is there a way he could have gone around, in a circle perhaps, and got to the prison block?'

'No, sir, not without passing the squad 'oo were over at the end o' the intrenchment, sir.'

'And Private Carpenter?'

'He was opposite me, working with Corporal Reilly.'

'All the time?'

'Yes, sir.'

'Thank you.' Busby turned to Narraway with a slight, ironic gesture of invitation.

Narraway accepted, playing for time rather than because he had any questions in mind. He hoped that something might come to him. Strafford's testimony had shown Tallis to be exactly the sort of man Narraway had thought him: brave, irreverent, with a completely irresponsible sense of humour, and intensely

112

compassionate, dedicated to medicine. It was also damning because he clearly would have found any other answer, if he could have.

Narraway stood facing Private Scott. Detail by detail he took time over every move he had described. He repeated what he had said before, not parrot fashion as if learned by rote, but clearly seeing it again in his mind's eye. Narraway achieved nothing at all.

It was exactly the same with Corporal Reilly, and then with Private Carpenter. Busby asked each of them where they had been. They each gave a sober account, in very slightly different words but amounting to the same evidence. In each case they supported each other, proving that none of them could have left their position, and the other's sight, long enough to have reached the prison block and gone inside it. He began to feel as if he was wasting everyone's time, and he could see the growing impatience in their faces.

Tallis was looking more and more desperate, struggling to keep his composure and an appearance of some kind of hope. Narraway could only guess the courage that required. Was he wasting everyone's time, drawing out the tension and the pain, pointlessly?

He thought of what Strafford had said of that terrible crossing with the boats on fire, the drowning and the dead, and Tallis wading in and risking his own life, without a backward glance. Narraway could not give up yet, not until he was so beaten he had nowhere else to go.

Lance-Corporal McLeod came to the stand

and Strafford questioned him also.

'Yes, sir,' McLeod said gravely. He was perhaps twenty-two, fair-skinned, pale. His eyes were hollow, staring far beyond Busby as if he saw something else, something printed indelibly on his memory.

Busby prompted him again. 'And where were you exactly, Corporal McLeod?'

'On the corner, sir, just beyond the building that was pretty well smashed.'

'To the south-west, correct?'

'Yes, sir.'

'And you could see the door to the prison from where you were?'

'Yes, sir.'

'Were you looking at it all the time?'

'No, sir. I was paying attention to what I was doing.'

'Which was what, Corporal?'

'Mending a cart, sir. Shaft was broken.'

'Was anyone helping you?'

'Yes, sir, Private Avery. Too heavy for one man, at least when it comes to lifting it together to weld.'

'And could you see Corporal Reilly and Private Scott working on the storeroom?'

'Yes, sir.'

'All the time? Are you certain?'

'Corporal Reilly could have gone the other way, sir, but not past me towards the prison, sir. Private Avery or me would have seen him.'

'Thank you. Please stay there so that Lieutenant Narraway can ask you . . . whatever it is he needs to.' Busby's invitation was palpable in the air. He did not hide the fact that he regarded this as a cruel and pointless waste not only of time but also of emotion. All around them was the air of danger, of hate, the bitter knowledge that fighting was going on just beyond their hearing and sight. All of northern India was in turmoil. Friends, allies, other men in a common cause, were dying to save what was left of British rule, and they were locked up in this tiny room angry over a truth everyone knew perfectly well. All it really needed was to be faced, and the bitter acceptance made and dealt with. Courage was necessary: not more talk, more weighing and measuring of what they all knew. In a sense it was like vultures fighting over a corpse. Busby had not said so, not in so many words, but he had more than implied it.

Narraway did not ask McLeod anything. He knew he had tried Latimer's patience as far as it would go.

The last witness was Private Avery.

Busby stood and faced him patiently.

'Private, would you describe to us exactly where you were at the time you knew Chuttur Singh was killed. We have been over this before. All you need to do is recall what you told me then, and tell me again, so the Court can hear you.'

Obediently, as if he were reciting some ritual litany, Avery told him exactly where he had been and what had occupied him. He seemed stunned. Narraway thought that the man blamed himself for not having seen something that could have saved Chuttur Singh, as if it had been his fault that he had been so near, and seen and done nothing to prevent the killing.

When it was Narraway's turn to question him, he felt brutal even to ask him to repeat it.

'Think carefully, Private Avery, and be certain that you have not left anything out. There is no need for you to say it all again.'

'Nothing, sir,' Avery answered. 'That's how it was. I'm sorry, sir.'

'Just one thing that Captain Busby didn't ask you. Do you know Corporal Tallis?'

Avery's face went even paler. 'Yes, sir.'

'How do you know him?'

'I got a bullet wound in the arm, sir. Not very bad, but it bled a lot. Corporal Tallis stitched it up for me.'

'Corporal Tallis did, not Dr Rawlins?' Narraway said with surprise.

'Dr Rawlins was busy with someone a lot worse hurt than me, sir.'

'I see. Did Corporal Tallis make a good job of it?'

'Yes, sir, very good. Healed up real well. And . . . ' He stopped; looked at the floor. 'There was a lot of blood, sir. I was scared. He made me laugh, and I felt as if it would be all right. It — it was the first time I'd been hit . . . sir.'

'So you know Corporal Tallis?'

'Yes, sir.' Avery looked so wretched it was as if he were in physical pain.

'Could you see the door of the prison from where you were working?'

'Yes, sir.'

'Did you see him during that hour? Did you

see him anywhere near the prison?'

'No, sir.'

'Thank you.' Narraway sat down again because he could think of nothing further that would not make it even worse.

Latimer adjourned the Court and Narraway walked out into the late afternoon. The sun was sinking low to the horizon, painting the west with burning colour. The coming night had already shrouded the east and was spreading a veil of shadow across the sky. He felt as if the darkness were enclosing him, wrapping around him and reaching inside.

It was a time not to be alone.

And yet only in solitude could he even attempt to concentrate his mind. Nothing so far helped. Every piece of testimony proved that no one else could have gone in through the prison door. And more than that, no one had an ill word to say about Tallis. None of them wished to believe him guilty.

Strafford's evidence had been even worse than Rawlins'. He was a good man desperately bereaved, who had nevertheless gone on doing his duty without expecting anyone else to ease his burden. He had not wanted Tallis to be guilty. It betrayed everything he had trusted, even the past help that Tallis had been to him personally. Perhaps he resented even more for the other men in his command — who were younger, less experienced — the fact that Tallis had also deceived them, maybe even broken their faith.

Did he doubt his own judgement, that he

could have been so wrong? If he could trust and admire a man, and be so bitterly mistaken, could he have faith in himself in any other judgement? If Tallis could be so infinitely less than his estimation, then who else might also be?

And if Strafford, with his knowledge, could be wrong, why on earth did Narraway imagine that he was any better? He barely knew Tallis. He liked his humour, and admired his courage. Strafford had known the man, day in day out, for years. He had seen his work. They faced horror and the final, rending grief of loss together, and he had also had the courage to accept that Tallis was guilty. What must that have cost him?

He could not shake the evidence. No one was lying, no combination of men had conspired to make the situation look this way. Wanting another answer was making him search for something that did not exist.

Perhaps Strafford was not being sarcastic when he said he had chosen Narraway because he believed in his stubbornness and his intelligence. Maybe he really did, and far from ending up feeling furious and duped, if Narraway could find a way out, a way to restore their faith in Tallis, and thus in their own judgement, Strafford would be intensely grateful?

So in failing, he was not only letting Tallis die, but failing the whole regiment — Strafford just as much. It was a lonely and terrible thing to live on without the faith you had once leaned on when all else broke under your weight. Death might not be preferable, but there must be times, at two o'clock in the morning, when it seemed a whole lot easier.

And there were women and children left without their men — like the one whose shopping he had carried, and whose little girl had given him her blue paper chain, made for a Christmas her son had said was for everybody.

Then suddenly he was ashamed of his own self-absorption. Whoever was betrayed, bereaved, accused falsely or not, it was not he. He was supposed to be part of the resolution, the one who fought for justice, whether that was Tallis's vindication or his death.

He was still walking, aimlessly. He had intended to go to his own house and spend the evening revising all that he had learned so far, in the hope that some inconsistency would emerge or some new fact or deduction appear.

However, as he walked along the road he found himself turning aside from the way to his own bungalow and going instead towards the house of the widow with the little girl who had given him the blue paper chain.

It was almost dusk and night would come quickly, as it always did in India. There was no lingering twilight of the north here. Soon there would be lights in the windows. Women would begin to cook an evening meal. The comfortable smells of food would fill the air. It would only be after the children had gone to bed that they would sit in the empty rooms downstairs and face the long aloneness of the night, the memories and the loss.

Helena was sitting on the front steps, holding

a doll in her arms and talking to it. She became aware of him standing at the gate and looked up. She smiled at him shyly.

He remained where he was, smiling back at her.

The woman came to the door. He had learned that her name was Olivia Barber. Perhaps she had seen him from the window and had come to make sure her child was safe.

'Good evening, Lieutenant,' she said clearly enough for him to hear her from where he was.

'Good evening, ma'am,' he replied. 'I beg your pardon for disturbing you.'

'It's supper time,' Helena said, still staring at him. 'Are you here for supper?'

He felt embarrassed, as if he had tried to invite himself in.

Olivia put her hand on the child's shoulder, pulling her back a little. 'You are welcome to supper, if you would like, Lieutenant,' she said quietly. 'I apologise for Helena's forwardness.'

He felt even more awkward, but he very much wanted to accept. He wanted the comfort, the normality of it, to think of life, and even of Christmas. She would do that, for her children's sake, whatever her own needs, or even pain that crushed her where no one else could see. If she wept, she would do it alone.

'Are you sure it will not inconvenience you?' he asked hesitantly. He too would love, above all else, to forget defeat for an hour or two.

'I'm quite sure,' she answered, opening the door a little wider behind her.

He went up the path and inside, Helena

watching him carefully all the way. He wondered with a flash of pain if she understood yet that her father was never coming home. Was she too young for that? Had her mother even tried to explain it?

Inside the house was warm and tidy, full of the smells of cooking, clean laundry and some kind of polish. There were a few toys on the floor, not many. He was pleased to see that there was no wagon. But then perhaps at five, David was too big for such things? Should he ask, or was that clumsy?

The food was not ready yet. He was invited to sit down.

'Aren't you going to play with me?' Helena looked disappointed. 'David's reading.'

'Helena!' Olivia said chidingly. 'The lieutenant has been working all day. He's tired.'

Helena's face crumpled with disappointment.

'I'd love to play with you,' Narraway said quickly. 'What game would you like?'

He was rewarded with a beaming smile. 'Hide and seek,' she said immediately.

'Helena . . . ' her mother began, but Helena was already running away, giggling with excitement.

Narraway stood up. 'Where should I look for her?' he asked quietly. 'I don't want to find her too soon. Please tell me where it's all right for me to try.'

Olivia laughed and gave a slight shrug. 'Anywhere in this half of the house,' she replied. 'You're fairly safe to try behind all the doors and in the cupboards. She hardly ever hides there.'

'Thank you.' He set off uncertainly. This was a house in which he was a guest, a woman's house, full of personal and family things. It would be inexcusable to intrude. To start with he moved tentatively, silently, then he realised it would be no fun for Helena if she could not hear him looking, puzzled, not finding her.

'I'm coming to find you!' he said clearly. He went out into the central entranceway. 'I think you're in the coat cupboard.' He opened the door, and was relieved to see nothing but coats and capes. He closed it again and saw a boot box. 'Could you be in there?' he said. 'Far too small — but maybe!' He opened it, sighed, and closed it again. 'No. Then where can you be?'

He kept it up, with a running commentary, going to one room after another, and still not finding her. Finally there was only one room left, which was clearly her bedroom. He opened it tentatively, afraid of intruding.

'She can't be in here,' he said aloud. 'It isn't bedtime yet.' He looked around. The small bed was neatly made, except for a coverlet dropped on the floor. She wasn't here. He was perplexed. He thought he had looked everywhere that had been suggested, excluding only the other bedrooms — Olivia's and the one where David was reading.

'I give up!' he said dramatically. 'She's gone!'

There was a giggle from the coverlet on the floor and very slowly a tousled little girl squirmed out of it, leaving it in exactly the same shape. Her face was alight with victory, eyes shining.

'I won!' she said happily. 'You didn't find me! I'm hungry. Are you coming for supper?' Dancing from one foot to the other, she led the way.

Narraway followed her out into the dining room and took his place at the table, opposite David, already there. He joined in, still a little awkwardly. He appreciated the welcome but he was acutely aware that he was in another man's place. So much of the warmth was a pretending, to comfort them all for a short space. It was a game that gave a few hours' respite from reality.

They spoke of other times and places, not India. Anything but the present. Christmas, with its promise of hope for those with the courage to accept its message and believe it.

But when the housemaid came to take David and Helena to bed, and they had all said good night, Narraway remained a little longer sitting in the quiet room. Now that pretence had ended, he could see how tired Olivia was, what an effort it cost her always to hide her grief from them, so they would not know how much everything had changed. War raged around them in every direction, but they were not afraid because, to them, she was not.

Suddenly his own troubles seemed very small, and very brief.

'Thank you,' he said sincerely. 'You have reminded me of the sanity of the things that last, and that they are not always bought cheaply.'

She looked at him in surprise, not quite sure what he meant. The meal had been simple, mostly rice.

He seized on the first thing that came to his mind. 'Have you any more garlands, paper chains? Perhaps I can help you put them up?'

'Lieutenant, they're only . . .'

'It'll need two of us,' he pointed out. 'One at each end. Wouldn't the children like to see them all up, when they come in in the morning?'

'You don't have to . . .' she began.

'I'd like to. We shouldn't ever forget Christmas, or make little of it. We give presents where we can, but there's no gift as precious as Christmas itself. It's belief.' He stopped, feeling self-conscious.

She smiled at him and stood up. 'You're quite right. Of course it is. I'd love you to help to put the garlands up. We have five or six, and there are some wreaths of dried flowers, and ribbons.'

She fetched them and together they put them up with pins and tacks, not always very straight, but an hour later, when it was finished, the room was transformed. There was a bright, slightly coloured courage to it, and as far as Narraway was concerned, it was like nailing your flags to the mast, a statement of hope.

'Do you think they'll like it?' he asked, looking carefully at her face, seeing the light in it again, even moments of laughter.

'They'll love it,' she said without hesitation. 'I think I shall pretend to be as surprised as they'll be, if you don't mind?'

'An excellent idea,' he agreed. 'We should prepare for Christmas, but it's good to know it will come anyway.'

'I'm thinking,' she said with a smile, 'would

you like a cup of tea before you go?'

'Thank you, I really would,' he accepted, following her into the kitchen while she made it, and the maid finished clearing away.

Afterwards, thanking her again, Narraway went out into the darkness, smiling. He would like to think that he had helped a little.

Far above him a flight of birds crossed the clear sky and circled down towards the trees. There always seemed to be birds, except over the ruined part of the town, lots of different kinds, unfamiliar to him. He loved their easy flight, which gave an illusion of freedom, an almost magical ability to rise above anything, and be wherever or whatever you wished.

He knew perfectly well they were as subject to hunger, cold, exhaustion and predators as anyone else, but the momentary dream was still worth something.

He would have to call all the witnesses again and find some discrepancy, some error or contradiction. He hated the thought of arguing and trying to trip them and find fault. The only thing that would be worse was letting Tallis be hanged without giving it the best fight he could.

And that brought him to the fact that he could no longer put off going to see Tallis, perhaps for the last time. The wind was rising a little and rustled the leaves on the trees that still held them, whispering, murmuring. It was nearly dark, no more birds left in the sky, just a thin ribbon of red fading in the west.

And then suddenly he had an idea, tremulous as the last light, elusive, but perhaps possible!

★　★　★

For a few moments he thought the tired guard would refuse to allow him in. However, he looked again at Narraway's face, at his eyes, and decided arguing with him would be a great deal more trouble than simply giving in.

Tallis was lying on his back on the bunk, eyes wide open. He stood up as Narraway came in and the door closed behind him. He was even paler than before, and there were bruises on his skin as if the flesh were already damaged.

'You look terrible,' Narraway said with some concern. 'Can I get Rawlins for you?'

Tallis's face broke into a smile. 'I like your sense of humour, Lieutenant. I couldn't have done better than that myself. To do what? You have to wait until the patient is dead before you certify it. Or have you given up on proving me innocent and you're going to smuggle me out as already dead, and say I escaped? Stupid, but I like a man who doesn't know when he's beaten.' He gave a mock salute.

Narraway heard the edge in his voice, the fear just under the surface. 'I was actually going to suggest that he give you something to make you look better, even if you don't feel it,' he replied, making an effort to smile back. 'I intend to finish the course, whether there's any point to it or not. It's one thing to be beaten, it's another to give up.'

'It won't do your career any good,' Tallis observed.

'Sit down before you fall over,' Narraway told

126

him. 'I may need your answers tomorrow.'

'It won't make any difference,' Tallis assured him. 'In civilian life they think twice about hanging a sick man, but in the army they don't give a damn. You can be missing arms and legs and out cold, some helpful bastard'll tie you up so they can still put the noose around your neck.'

'Thank you,' Narraway said wryly. 'If I'm ever accused back at home, I'll remember to be ill at the time. Now sit down and try to pay attention.'

Tallis sat. In fact, it was more of an overbalancing because he had temporarily forgotten there was no chair, only the mattress on the ground. He looked up at Narraway, a flare of hope in his eyes for a moment, before he remembered to disguise it.

'Did you kill Chuttur Singh?' Narraway asked.

'No.'

'What do you know about Dhuleep? And don't tell me 'nothing'. You've treated half the men in this regiment. I need you to tell me everything you know about him, whether you think it's relevant or not. I don't care if it's military, personal or medical. It's not just your life depending on it, it's a matter of finding the man who did kill Chuttur, if it isn't you. It's about saving some kind of honour for the regiment.'

Tallis looked amazed. Then laughter welled up in him, and died instantly.

'No,' he said croakily. 'I'm not noble enough to swing on a rope for a crime I didn't commit, if that's what you think. I don't want to be executed out here and my name go down as a traitor.' He blinked rapidly, trying to stop his eyes filling with tears. 'I don't want my family to live with that . . . my mother. She was once . . . terribly proud of me . . . '

Narraway found his own throat tight. He refused to allow thoughts of his last parting with his mother. She was slender and dark, as he was. She was also a woman of immense elegance and quiet, very private passion, again, as he was.

'Then tell me!' he said in sudden fury, sitting down on the floor opposite Tallis. 'Tell me everything you know about Chuttur Singh and Dhuleep Singh. And be quick. I've only got tonight, and I'd like to get enough sleep to be able to stand up in court and not have to have anyone prop me up. It won't make any difference if you collapse, it might if I do!'

'No, it won't,' Tallis said quickly. 'Not really. It'll just look silly.'

'Now, Corporal!' Narraway snapped. 'Tell me every last detail you know about Dhuleep and Chuttur. You've got until midnight.'

'What are you going to do at midnight?' Tallis asked curiously. 'You need a hell of a lot of sleep, for a young and supposedly healthy soldier.'

'I'm going to find out more about these men myself, and put the pieces together, of course! Make a different picture. Get on with it.'

But Tallis could tell him little more than he already knew, only paint more vividly the horror and the exhaustion. There was no anger in him, except at the circumstances that cost young men so much of their lives, and seemingly for so little in return. There was pity and wry, twisting humour, snatches of companionship, gulfs of loneliness, and always at the back of it a courage that climbed up to its feet every time it was beaten down.

But nothing Tallis said made the new theory in Narraway's mind impossible, and just after midnight he began finding the men himself, waking them up if necessary, asking questions over and over again.

What had Dhuleep been like as a soldier, as a man? Obviously he was a Sikh, that much was clear from his name. Some Sikhs had remained loyal to the British, some had joined the mutiny. Why had he changed sides, and — what was more urgent — why had no one noticed?

Was he guilty of the charge for which he was in prison?

'That — and theft earlier on,' one weary sergeant told him, sitting half asleep in the canteen. He was blinking at Narraway with a better temper than Narraway would have shown, woken up at two in the morning by some man senior to him in rank, but years junior in experience.

'Theft of what?' Narraway asked.

'Medicines, I think,' the sergeant replied. 'Quinine, stuff like that.'

'To sell? To use on others? Did he need it himself?' Narraway was interested because it was an indication of Dhuleep's character and opportunism.

'Not that much!' the sergeant said with a twisted smile. 'God knows what he wanted it for. He wouldn't say. Could have been to sell, or to take to the mutineers, to give to his friends or allies, or simply to rob us of the use of it.'

'Could Tallis have been in on it?' It was a question he really did not want the answer to, but he dared not evade it. 'For profit?' he added.

'No,' the sergeant said without hesitation. 'It was Tallis who reported the theft. If he'd waited we probably wouldn't have known who did it, or got it back, for that matter.'

'So you caught Dhuleep Singh because of Tallis?'

'I suppose so. But it wasn't Tallis as got 'im, it was a couple of regulars called . . . Johnson was one of 'em, I think the other was Robinson, or Roberts. Something like that.'

'What sort of a man was Dhuleep, before the theft?'

'Dunno. Ordinary, I think. Bit of a sneaky sod, but a good enough soldier. At least he seemed that way. If 'e ever stole before, 'e got away with it.'

'Why was there only one guard looking after Dhuleep?' Narraway asked.

''Cos 'e were just a miserable layabout, an' 'e were locked up tight in a cell anyway. Probably wouldn't 'ave bothered even then, if it 'adn't been the medicines 'e took before, an' we never really did 'im for.'

'Thank you.' Narraway stood up. 'I'd better go and look over all this past evidence and see if I can make anything different of it.'

The sergeant stood as well, a big man, broad-chested, his shoulders sagging with weariness. 'Ye're a tryer, I'll say that for yer.

Don't give up, do yer!'

'Not till it's over,' Narraway answered, finding the praise both bitter, and welcome.

★ ★ ★

An hour later, Narraway had gone yet again over all the evidence he had when he suddenly came across what looked like an inconsistency between what Corporal Reilly had said, and Private Carpenter's account. It was very tiny: just something in the order of events, none of which mattered in themselves. He looked at his notes again, reread them to make sure it was not his own hasty writing misleading him.

Corporal Reilly had said that he had been standing on the corner where he could see Scott on the far side of the courtyard, planing the wood for the new door, and McLeod and Avery in the corner opposite, with a clear view of the prison entrance a hundred yards away to their left.

He also said that Carpenter had been there all the time with him, as borne out by all three of the others.

But if Reilly was right, and his account matched Scott's, then Carpenter was lying. He had backed up McLeod and Avery when they must actually have been out of his sight, in the direction of the prison. It was very small, but they could not all be correct. Was it just an error: by a man too tired, too shaken to remember accurately? Did it even matter now? Not if his own idea was right. But what if it were not? He could not afford to rely on it. If it were wrong, he must have something to fall back on. They had all sworn that their time was accounted for, and no one else could have gone into the prison before Grant led the response to the alarm.

He must waken Carpenter right now, and get some explanation. It was harsh to disturb the man in the middle of the night to tax him with what might be no more than an error, but Tallis's life could depend on it.

Narraway crossed the open space to remnants of the barracks where Carpenter was billeted and found him with some difficulty. He had to persuade a guard of who he was and that his errand could not wait. He expected to find Carpenter asleep. Instead the man was lying uncomfortably on a straw mattress, tossing fitfully. He sat up as soon as he was aware of Narraway's presence in the room.

Narraway apologised immediately. He kept his voice as quiet as he could make it, so as not to disturb the other men who were within earshot, and might also sleep lightly.

'I need to speak to you before the trial resumes tomorrow. Privately.'

'What?' Carpenter was dazed. 'Lieutenant? You're going to call me again?' He pushed his hand through his hair and sat up a little further. 'What for? I've no idea who killed Chuttur Singh. I just know it wasn't me, and it wasn't Reilly, or Scott. Couldn't have been.'

'Can we go outside?' Narraway asked. He phrased it as a request, but it was in effect an order.

In silence Carpenter stood up, pulled on his trousers and tunic and followed Narraway outside into the night. It was dark. Even the clear sky's blaze of stars gave little light, and the wind was higher than before, scraping the branches and rattling the leaves on the tamarind trees twenty feet away.

'What is it, sir?' Carpenter asked, shivering a little.

Narraway went over Carpenter's evidence step by step. He knew it by heart now. He repeated every moment, every word that accounted for someone else. Did it matter? He had no idea. He could not afford to let anything slip.

'Yes,' Carpenter said wearily.

Narraway shook his head. 'No,' he denied quietly. 'Not if Corporal Reilly was where he said, doing what he said. He would have been around the corner, out of sight of the prison. It can't be right. One of you has it wrong. Is that a mistake, or a lie? Think carefully before you decide, Private.'

Carpenter stood motionless. Narraway's eyes were used to the dark, but even so he could see no expression on Carpenter's face. He blinked several times, as if the dust eddies troubled him. Once he rubbed his arm over his face.

Narraway waited. He felt guilty. There was no arrogance, no anger in the man in front of him, just an inner conflict he could not resolve.

'If you don't tell me the truth, Tallis may be hanged for something he didn't do,' he said at last. 'A good man, a man we need, will suffer an injustice we can't ever put right. Was it a mistake,

Private Carpenter, or a lie?'

Carpenter chewed his lip.

Again Narraway waited. He thought for a moment that Carpenter had fallen asleep on his feet.

'It was a lie, sir.' Carpenter's voice in the dark was painful, as if his mouth were too dry to form the words properly.

'Did you leave, or did Reilly?' Narraway asked, chilled now that what had been only a possibility — a straw to reach for — had become a reality.

'Reilly did, sir,' Carpenter replied. 'At least as far as I know, he did.' He straightened up until his body was stiff. 'I didn't see anything relevant to Chuttur Singh's murder, sir. Nor did I see Corporal Tallis, or Dhuleep Singh after his escape. I can't help with what happened, sir.'

Narraway found he was shivering too. Was there any point in pressing this? Would it make any difference to Tallis? Not if his own idea was right. But the more he thought of it, clearly, the wilder it seemed.

'I still want to know where you were,' he said aloud.

Carpenter looked resigned, beaten. 'I was with Ingalls, sir. He was . . . ill.'

'Then Major Rawlins would know that,' Narraway reasoned, wondering why Rawlins had said nothing earlier. Was it possible he did not know of Carpenter's testimony? Considering the tension, the grief and the anger at the murder of Chuttur Singh, and Dhuleep's betrayal of the patrol, then Strafford's questioning of everyone's whereabouts, that seemed hard to believe.

'Private Carpenter!' he said sharply.

'Yes, sir?' Carpenter stiffened.

' "Yes, sir, Rawlins knows of this", or just, 'Yes, sir, I am paying attention'?' Narraway demanded.

'Yes, sir . . . I am paying attention. No, sir, Major Rawlins doesn't know. It was . . . it wasn't that kind of illness . . . '

'You mean he was drunk? Why didn't he just sleep it off, like anyone else?' Narraway was puzzled, even disturbed. Was he about to learn the truth of Chuttur's murder after all? 'Carpenter! You are better to tell me the truth now rather than have me drag it out of you, and this Ingalls, in court in a few hours' time.'

'Yes, sir.' Carpenter's body sagged as if he no longer had the strength or the will to stand upright.

Narraway took him by the arm. His flesh was cold even through his tunic. 'Here. For God's sake come and sit down, and tell me what was wrong with Ingalls, and why you went to him rather than call a doctor.'

Carpenter stopped resisting. Together they walked over to a pile of rubble still lying piled up from the bombardment of the siege. For a moment or two he sat bent forward, composing his thoughts, then he began to speak.

'Ingalls drinks . . . badly. He was right out of it that day. Jones covered for him. We do.' He did not even look at Narraway to challenge him. 'But he couldn't handle this. Ingalls was worse than usual. He was shaking like a leaf and sobbing. Jones couldn't keep him from yelling out. In his own mind he was miles away, in another world, back in the time when we first came in after the siege. He was one of the ones who found the bodies in the well in the Bibighar. They swore on oath then, and he thinks he's betrayed it because he . . . ' He stopped, lowering his head into his hands.

'What?' Narraway asked, feeling brutal. He was afraid of what he was going to hear. 'I have to know if I'm going to help Tallis,' he insisted.

'He was delirious,' Carpenter said. 'He could see it all again, smell the blood, hear the flies. Tallis helped him sometimes. Made him laugh.' He twisted around to face Narraway for a moment. 'You've got to help Tallis, sir. I don't know what the hell happened, but he couldn't have done it, unless he had a reason, I mean one he couldn't get out of, one that . . . ' He turned away again and fell silent.

'Ingalls,' Narraway prodded him.

'He was out of it,' Carpenter said. 'He was going to kill himself. Said he'd failed. General Wheeler's daughter was haunting him. He could see her ghost everywhere.'

'What?' Narraway gasped. 'General Wheeler's daughter? What are you talking about, man? Failed her? General Wheeler?' His mind whirled with lunatic possibilities. 'Carpenter!'

Carpenter looked at him.

'Why you?' Narraway demanded.

'Because I was there too.'

'Where?'

'In the Bibighar. She was one of the women they killed. We found her head. Somebody — I think it was Frazer — cut off her scalp and divided it up, a piece of it to every man. He told us to count the hairs on our piece, and swear on oath to kill one mutineer for every hair. Ingalls couldn't do it. He tried . . . '

Narraway sat frozen, unaware of everything around him, the night wind in the tamarind branches, the dust devils stirring across the open ground, the starlight.

Carpenter moved a little, just shifting position. 'What have we become, sir? He doesn't understand. He asks over and over again what the hell we're doing here anyway. Never mind making the Indians into Christians, what are we making ourselves? And you know what, sir? I can't answer him. I don't know what to do! Tell you the truth, I wished Tallis was there. He knew what to say, 'cos he'd make fun of it all, not try to be right, just be . . . gentle.'

Narraway sat without moving or speaking. He wanted to save Tallis so badly it was like a physical pain inside him, an ache as if something necessary for survival were missing, and the emptiness was going to eat him away.

'He wouldn't even tell you you were going to live, if you were going to die, and he knew it,' Carpenter went on, his voice seeming almost disembodied in the darkness and the sound of the tamarind trees rattling in the wind. 'He didn't even seem to believe in much. Never talked about it. But if you were scared out of your wits, or so drunk you couldn't stand up, and seeing all kinds of things that weren't there, and run away like an idiot, sit angry in a corner, hugging your knees, an' can't stop crying, he'd still talk to you like a man, and you were worth something.'

'How long did you stay with Ingalls?' Narraway asked.

'Don't know. Until he calmed down and I was sure he'd sleep it off, and not cut his throat. Couldn't very well hide all the knives, could I?' He gave a sharp burst of laughter. 'Tallis said that once: 'Let's hide all the knives and guns so no one'll kill themselves. Course, then they won't be able to kill each other either, but there are no perfect answers, eh?' And then he gave that crazy laugh of his.' He let out a long sigh. 'But that doesn't help, does it? I'd have sworn my life he'd never hurt anyone, but maybe he went mad and did it. Reilly was there, and Scott only lied to save me. And I lied to save Ingalls. Makes no difference to the fact that no one but Tallis could have got in there, because he was still the only one who had the chance.'

He turned to Narraway, sitting up straighter. 'Pity you can't hang Ingalls instead. He'd like it. It'd put him out of his misery. Tallis would've said that, and laughed. Except it's not funny, 'cos it's true. I can't help you, sir. And you should believe that, because if I could've helped, I'd have done it already.'

'I'm sorry for waking you,' Narraway said quietly. 'I thought for a few moments that I'd find something. Go back to bed. You might sleep. You have to some time.'

For several more moments Carpenter did not move, then at last he rose to his feet, stiffly.

'Sorry, sir,' he said again, and before Narraway could reply, he stumbled away into the shadows and was lost.

Narraway sat uncomfortably on the rubble a few moments longer, then he stood up and walked slowly through the darkness and the cold, rising wind towards his own quarters, and a few hours of oblivion before the battle.

★ ★ ★

The next morning was still and cold. It had never been known to snow in Cawnpore, but it was easy to believe that the shortest day of the year was coming, and Christmas would be only a few days afterwards.

The small room was grim. No one looked as if they had slept, and the very idea of celebrating anything like Christmas seemed absurd, an idea belonging to a different world.

Busby stood up.

'I have no more witnesses to call, sir,' he addressed Latimer but included the other two officers in his gaze. 'There is no question that Chuttur Singh was hacked to death, and I have demonstrated beyond any doubt that there was no one else who could have done it, except Corporal John Tallis. I cannot offer any explanation for why he did so. Whether he was threatened, or bribed, or simply lost his sanity under the pressure of events, I don't know, nor do I believe that it matters. The facts remain.'

Latimer nodded slowly, his face furrowed deep with unhappiness. He turned to Narraway. 'Do you have anything you would like to say, or to ask, Lieutenant Narraway? It is your duty to offer anything you can on behalf of the prisoner.'

Narraway stood up slowly. His brief sleep had been full of nightmares and he felt as if this were little more than an extension of the suffocating failure he already felt. His mouth was dry.

'Yes, sir.' He swallowed. 'Captain Busby has presented a powerful case for Corporal Tallis's guilt, but it rests solely on the fact that he was unable to find anyone else to blame. He has not even suggested that Corporal Tallis was seen at the time and the place, that he behaved like a guilty man, that he had any mark on him of a fight of any sort: bruises, cuts, blood, even a torn or stained uniform. He has given us no reason at all why Tallis should do such a thing, except out of complete insanity, which must have come on without warning, and went again without leaving any mark behind it. As Captain Busby admits, he simply has no one else to blame.'

Busby stood up.

'Sit down, Captain,' Latimer said grimly. 'Your disagreement is taken for granted. Give the man his chance.'

Busby's face tightened, but he did not speak again.

'Sir,' Narraway resumed, 'I believe there may be some explanation for all the facts we have, other than Corporal Tallis's guilt, but I need to question the witness again, very precisely, before I can be certain. I have already dismissed errors, which I investigated more closely, and found them to be unrelated to Chuttur Singh's death. I need now to explore certain other aspects that this may have thrown light upon.' That was something of an exaggeration. He had no intention of telling them about Carpenter and Ingalls, but he had to make it sound as if he had a better cause for recalling witnesses than speculation, however plausible.

Latimer hesitated, seemed about to say something, then changed his mind. 'Proceed, Lieutenant Narraway, but if you stray far from the point I shall stop you myself, never mind any objection Captain Busby may have.'

'Yes, sir. I call Corporal Grant again.'

Grant was duly reminded of his oath and faced Narraway looking puzzled.

Narraway was painfully aware of everyone in the room looking at him with displeasure and a degree of suspicion. He avoided meeting Tallis's eyes.

'Corporal Grant.' Narraway stopped and cleared his throat. Suddenly his whole idea seemed absurd. He was going to make a complete fool of himself, ruin his career, disappoint Latimer, see Tallis hanged. He cleared his throat again. 'Would you remind us where you were when you heard the prison alarm, and what you did. Please be absolutely exact, and if there is something you don't recall, say so. There is no shame in having your mind so bent in your duty, especially in times of emergency, that you don't notice other things.'

Grant did as he was asked, slowly and carefully.

When he had finished Narraway picked up the

thread again, his voice shaking a little.

'The dying Chuttur Singh told you that the prisoner had escaped,' he confirmed. 'He had valuable information regarding the patrol, and at all costs you should go after him. He himself was beyond help, even had you found a doctor for him, is that correct?'

'Yes, sir,' Grant agreed. 'I wanted to get help for Chuttur, but he insisted it was pointless, and I should go after the prisoner.' He looked distressed, his face flushed, as if now he felt guilty for his decision.

'And this was after Sergeant Attwood and Private Peterson had also arrived?' Narraway needed every last detail clear, exact. 'Was it dark in the room?' He held his breath for the answer. 'Chuttur's face splashed with blood?'

'Yes, sir.'

Busby rose to his feet, his face grim, his voice grating with anger.

'Sir, these men all did exactly what they were trained to do, and what was the right thing. To suggest now that they were somehow mistaken and should have stayed with a man who was beyond all help is cruel and quite wrong. It only displays Lieutenant Narraway's inexperience, and — '

Latimer held up his hand. 'Enough, Captain Busby. Your point is perfectly clear.' He turned to Narraway. 'Lieutenant, are you trying to suggest that any or all of these men should have tried to assist Chuttur Singh rather than go after the escaped prisoner? It was a judgement made in the heat of the moment, but I believe a correct one. Either way, what difference does it make to the guilt or innocence of John Tallis?'

Narraway felt the blood burn up his face. He knew he had sounded brutal, as if he were blaming Grant, but there was no other way. Please God he was right!

'No, sir,' he said, keeping his voice as steady as he could. 'Grant, Attwood and Peterson all behaved exactly as good soldiers should, sir. I intend no criticism at all. I just want to be absolutely certain, beyond any doubt at all, that that's what they did.'

'If you do not reach some point soon I shall be obliged to stop you, for wasting our time,' Latimer warned. 'Get on with it.'

Narraway turned to Grant again. 'All of you left in pursuit of the escaped prisoner, Dhuleep Singh? You are sure of that?'

'Yes, sir,' Grant repeated, his face pale, his distress obvious.

'Thank you. That's all,' Narraway said quietly. He hesitated on the edge of apology, and missed the chance.

Busby declined to ask Grant anything further. His expression reflected his disgust.

It was all hanging on one gamble now. Narraway stood up again. 'I would like to call Dr Rawlins back, sir.'

'Is that really necessary, Lieutenant?' Latimer asked wearily.

'Yes, sir. I believe he may be able to complete my defence of Corporal Tallis, sir,' Narraway answered. The hope was taking firmer and clearer shape in his mind all the time. If he were wrong, then there really was nothing left to say.

Latimer agreed. There was a long, tense silence while someone went to find Rawlins and bring him. Narraway stood simply because he was too tense to sit down. He did not dare look at Tallis. It was possibly cowardly of him, but the hope was so close, and yet still so far-fetched that he did not dare offer it.

Busby sat back in his chair, making no secret of his impatience and his contempt. He fidgeted, moved papers, twisted around to see if Rawlins were coming yet.

Latimer waited without moving or looking at either of the officers who sat with him. He seemed to be on the edge of exhaustion, as if hope had died in him too. His dark face was haggard.

The seconds crawled by.

Finally Rawlins arrived. Everyone sat up straight and forced themselves to listen.

Rawlins was reminded of his oath, and his position, and he waited with surprise to hear what Narraway wanted of him now. He too avoided looking at Tallis.

Narraway picked his words with intense care. Everything he said might hold the key to a man's life. He cleared his throat.

'Major Rawlins, you described the injuries to Chuttur Singh. I don't wish you to do so again. Please just confirm that they were as you told us before. He was struck on the head, but not seriously enough to kill him, just to stun? His body was slashed with deep sword wounds from which he bled profusely, so much so that his

144

uniform was sodden with blood. Is that accurate?'

Rawlins' face was tight, bleak with the memory. 'Yes.'

'He bled to death?' Narraway said.

'I've already said that.' Rawlins was angry. 'There was nothing I could have done to save him. To suggest otherwise is not only ridiculous, it is offensive to the three men who found him.'

'That would be Grant, Attwood and Peterson?' Narraway said. He was aware of an electric tension in the room, almost a prickling. Any moment now Busby was going to interrupt and break the spell. 'Doctor?' he prodded urgently.

'Yes, of course it was!' Rawlins snapped.

'The men went after Dhuleep, to see if they could recapture him?'

'Yes!' Rawlins was all but shouting.

'Then who was it who brought the body of Chuttur Singh to you?' Narraway's mouth was so dry he could barely form the words clearly, and yet his body was running with sweat.

Rawlins froze, his eyes wide.

There was a silence in the room that was all but suffocating, as if the air were too thick to breathe.

'Oh God!' Rawlins said in horror. 'It was a Sikh . . . it . . . '

Narraway licked his lips and forced his voice to be steady. 'Could it have been Dhuleep Singh, Captain Rawlins?'

Rawlins had known what he was going to say. He stared back at him with wide eyes in an ashen face.

'Yes, it could.'

Busby sat upright, staring.

Latimer leaned forward, looking first at Rawlins, then at Narraway.

Narraway swallowed hard.

'Sir,' he said to Latimer. 'I suggest that there is an alternative answer to this tragedy. John Tallis is as innocent of it as he has always claimed. The assumption that he is guilty arises only from the lack of any other answer.'

Now Busby was on his feet. 'Are you saying Dhuleep made his own escape, without Tallis's help? That's ridiculous! How did he get out? He was gone before Grant, Attwood or Peterson even got there.'

'No,' Narraway said firmly. 'No, he was not.' He turned back to Latimer. 'What if Dhuleep Singh tricked Chuttur, feigned illness, or offered information, or anything else. He attacked Chuttur and took his sword, and keys. Then when he had killed him he — '

'He was there when Grant got there!' Busby interrupted.

'No!' Narraway said again. 'Chuttur was stripped of his guard's uniform and left concealed by the pile of bedclothes. The man Grant spoke to, who told him Dhuleep had escaped, with vital information, was Dhuleep himself, with blood concealing his features, and wrapped in Chuttur's blood-stained clothes. We all assumed that someone had opened the door from the outside, and Dhuleep had escaped, closing it behind him. But in fact it was Grant who first opened the door.'

There was a sigh around the room, but not a soul moved.

'Dhuleep urged Grant and the others to go, as quickly as possible. As soon as they had done, he took off Chuttur's blood-soaked clothes and re-dressed him, and took him to Rawlins. Then he left to join the search — for himself! There was no third man.' He took a deep shuddering breath. 'That answers all the questions, sir, and it shows John Tallis to be guilty of nothing more than being the only one in the immediate area who happened to be working alone.'

Rawlins rubbed his hand across his brow. 'You're right,' he said with amazement, and a relief so intense his body shook with it, the colour surging back into his face. 'I barely looked at the man who brought Chuttur in; I had all my attention on the injured man. But he was a Sikh, and there was no one else unaccounted for except Tallis, and Dhuleep Singh.' His voice gained strength and urgency. 'But we thought Dhuleep had gone. Of course the three who went looking for him didn't catch him — he was behind them! He went out of the hospital door, in the opposite direction, and got clean away.' He looked across at Tallis. 'I'm sorry, John. I was so bloody horrified at what they'd done to Chuttur I never more than glanced at the man who brought him.'

'He was counting on that,' Narraway observed. Then he faced Latimer. 'Sir, I respectfully request that Corporal John Tallis be found not guilty of any wrongdoing at all. There is no villain here.'

Slowly Latimer smiled, the light coming back

147

into his eyes, the colour to his face. He straightened in his chair and looked first to the man on his right, then the man on his left. Each one nodded, smiling.

'Thank you, Lieutenant Narraway,' he said quietly. 'This Court finds Corporal John Tallis not guilty in any way whatsoever.' He looked at Tallis. 'You are free to go, Corporal.'

Tallis tried to stand, but he was too weak with the sudden, almost unbelievable turn in his fortunes, and his legs folded under him.

Strafford walked across the court to Narraway, holding out his hand.

'Strafford Minor was wrong about you,' he said with intense, burning pleasure. 'You're a damn good soldier. There won't be a man or a woman in the regiment who isn't grateful to you for this. You've given us back a belief in ourselves. Happy Christmas.'

Narraway felt tears sting his eyes. 'Thank you, sir. Happy Christmas to you also. I feel a bit more like celebrating now. In fact I'll go and put some decorations up in my quarters. I've got a blue paper garland I want to hang somewhere special.'

Strafford did not ask him to explain. Not that he would have. He simply took his hand and clasped it so hard he all but crushed his fingers.

'Thank you,' he said again. 'Happy Christmas.'

We do hope that you have enjoyed reading this large print book.

Did you know that all of our titles are available for purchase?

We publish a wide range of high quality large print books including:
Romances, Mysteries, Classics
General Fiction
Non Fiction and Westerns

Special interest titles available in large print are:
The Little Oxford Dictionary
Music Book
Song Book
Hymn Book
Service Book

Also available from us courtesy of Oxford University Press:
Young Readers' Dictionary
(large print edition)
Young Readers' Thesaurus
(large print edition)

For further information or a free brochure, please contact us at:
Ulverscroft Large Print Books Ltd.,
The Green, Bradgate Road, Anstey,
Leicester, LE7 7FU, England.
Tel: (00 44) 0116 236 4325
Fax: (00 44) 0116 234 0205

Other titles published by
The House of Ulverscroft:

A SUNLESS SEA

Anne Perry

1864 and on the bank of the Thames, the mutilated body of a woman is found on Limehouse Pier. Inspector William Monk's enquiries unearth a connection between the victim and Dr Lambourn. A recently deceased scientist, Lambourn was a supporter of a new pharmaceutical bill to regulate the sale of opium. Not all is as it seems, as Lambourn's widow refuses to believe the verdict of suicide. She is convinced that he was murdered after government officials, intent on keeping the lucrative trade of opium flowing, discredited his research. Pressure mounts for the river police to find the Limehouse killer, and Monk's investigation into the depths of the opium trade threatens to expose corruption in the very highest echelons of society . . .